A WISTFUL WANDERING

A WISTFUL WANDERING

ROHIT KHARE

PARTRIDGE
A Penguin Random House Company

ISBN:	Hardcover	978-1-4828-5600-2
	Softcover	978-1-4828-5599-9
	eBook	978-1-4828-5598-2

Because of the dynamic nature of the Internet, any web addresses or links contained in this book may have changed since publication and may no longer be valid. The views expressed in this work are solely those of the author and do not necessarily reflect the views of the publisher, and the publisher hereby disclaims any responsibility for them.

Print information available on the last page.

To order additional copies of this book, contact
Partridge India
000 800 10062 62
orders.india@partridgepublishing.com

www.partridgepublishing.com/india

Contents

for Mansi
(the one and only)

Dear Reader,

What began as a habit of entering my personal diary; slowly (over the long years) turned to a desire to have someone read it too. Hence, here you find it in your hands – my diary – with all its moles and warts.

I have to mention here my deep appreciation and gratitude to my Wife – Mansi, for having always supported me all through and reading patiently all that I needed her opinion upon. And thanks too, to my beautiful children – Khushboo and Dhruv for always encouraging me and together making all the lovely illustrations for this book. Without my family, this was simply a lost project.

Last of all, thanks dear Reader, for your trust in picking up this book and giving it a chance to make itself heard.

Best wishes,
Rohit Khare

The Mountains

(Once upon a time I met a man whose sole passion was climbing mountains. You could call him a compulsive trekker I guess. Since I have always lived in the city and have very little exposure to outdoors, I asked him how mountains really are and what it feels like climbing them. There came a sudden wistful look in his eyes and this is what he had to say)

'Having spent sufficient time in the mountains, I feel I know them a little better than most other folk. When I say mountains, I don't mean the tourist destinations such as Dehradun, Shimla or Nainital. I mean those real, rugged and desolate mountains which are located in the far and remote fringes of our country. When you come to think of it the mountains happen to be quite different from all other manifestations of nature; in particular, they are too stoic and bear all elements of weather and extremes of mercury in the most quiet and unassuming manner. Look at the oceans, they rise and fall with the phases of the moon; the rivers make so much noise as they rush through the boulders; the forests are changing with every change of season ; think of the winds – they howl so much. But come to the mountains - and you have these unchanging giants who never utter a word as they stand unaffected for centuries.

Whether you take up sailing, surfing, micro lite flying or scuba-diving; none of them I guess draws as much sweat as the mountains draw from you. Climbing any mountain requires deliberate planning - as to what you'll wear, carry or eat. Where you'll halt; where should you have reached by night fall and so on? You forget one little thing and it can abort your entire effort and may even endanger your life. All this adds further to the thrill and charm of mountains. From whatever distance you look at them they are looking back at you; and you can feel a challenge being cast at you in their loud yet silent voices. They dare you with their characteristic calm and serenity. Having climbed quite a bit of mountains myself, I retrospect that after a certain amount of climb there comes a threshold where each mountain having exhausted your energy reserves, dares you to climb further. It is the stage where your knees feel like jelly; your breath seems to be running out faster than the money in your bank; your chest feels ready to burst and other similar trepidations hit you all together. However if at this point you can turn a deaf ear to your body, keep yourself stable on your feet and somehow manage to walk a few more minutes; believe me, before you realize you would have crossed the threshold and achieved the critical mass required to explode your way to the top.

So each mountain tests you, your physical stamina and your mental fortitude. Mountains in a way can even grow on you like women – whom you don't really crave but have simply got used to - keeping away draws you back.

Slowly you start to enjoy the sheer exhaustion and the tremendous sweat they draw from you. As you tire, your mind swears never to climb a mountain again; but I have found this feeling to be very short lived and it goes away as soon as you have recovered your poise. When you are really tired in the middle of a climb, even a harmless gentle slope can convincingly give you the same painful pleasure as scaling the Kanchenjunga.

Every mountain seems beautiful from far, but only those who have climbed some of them - know the real labour involved in approaching and scaling such beauties. Generally in life, one side of the journey is always easy; but so far as climbing a mountain goes, getting down from it is equally tough. In fact, getting down a mountain can be even tougher; every single ounce of your body throws its full weight on the poor wobbling knees. Notwithstanding the pain and the sweat, the mountains quite often even evoke a soft romanticism in the human heart and stimulate philosophical musings.

I think the mountains and the clouds are the best of friends; you can always see them engrossed in a silent exchange of secrets over the peaks. Then there are those valleys and passes amidst the high mountains, which I think God made only to serve the purpose of a permanent abode to the clouds. At the end of a long day, you will invariably find the clouds coming back and settling into these valleys. In the morning they get up and carry-on to where ever they are supposed to be going; but always return by night fall without exception. In fact I like to believe that the same clouds live in the same valleys, from the moment they are born till they grow up and eventually die. Though on the face of it you might think that a mountain is a dead creature, but suddenly in a quiet spot you will find a bubbly spring breaking through its skin; reminding you that forces of nature are very much active beneath the hard exterior.

The mountains may be 'unchanging'; but quite like us they are prey to cosmetics. In winters, once snow-covered, they seem simple and honest. You can see far and clear. Come spring; the snow melts and vegetation abounds - the same mountains become thick with undergrowth and heavy foliage; they now seem full of mysteries and hide more than what they reveal.

You can never take the mountains for granted; you have got to learn their language. Taking them lightly can cost you your life. Yes, the mountains are surely difficult creatures to know; but once you strike a rapport, you just can't let go. They beckon you and you will see yourself succumb time and again, despite the swearing and the sweat.'

I Don't Care

(There was once this psycho-therapist or a real life coach as she liked to call herself. She had a host of problems of her own (you know how it is). For quite some time she tried to straighten things out for herself. But when it just didn't work out, she simply closed the door and walked away without any baggage. Now she helps other people figure out things full time (because she's seen how it can't be done alone). She doesn't charge any money; it brings her peace she says. Back in the days when I met her, she was helping people return from recklessness. And this is what she told me, when we got talking)

'Have you ever wondered why so many people lead utterly reckless lives? By reckless I mean being reckless with themselves, and having a total disregard for their health and safety. The type of stuff I am talking about could be smoking endless cigarettes, doing drugs, dope, grass, cannabis, excessive alcohol or any other type of imaginable or unimaginable substances. Some even sniff glue or gulp endless amounts of cough syrup.

Also included is dangerous driving, sex addiction, bingeing on unhealthy foods and whatever or whichever activity gives such a person an instant kick or self-gratification. Sometimes these people may hover too dangerously close to the precipice. It is more than a simple addiction; it is in fact a serious disorder which needs a closer look. Such living at times also brings one's family and close ones within the realm of dangerousness and exposes them to similar risks as the person in question himself. However the one person is so myopic and obsessed with the infliction that he or she is unable to fathom this.

I prefer to call such living as self-abuse and when observed closely, the person concerned is so totally self-centered and selfish in his obsession; that he doesn't care to, nor has any time to think of anything else - other than the kick he wants to draw for himself all the time. I guess a person reaches such a point in time when due to certain reasons or chain of events he or she comes to see no gain in living or no loss in dying. He lives with the only aim of making each moment more gripping, ecstatic, dangerous or whatever it is which gives him the kick.

Such a situation possibly presents when the individual sees no future, or even knowing, has no craving to get there. Just imagine the sickness of the situation when you feel no craving for the future. This happens when you feel that getting there won't make anything better for you. Though you might see more money or comforts for yourself there, but it all fails to inspire a desire within your heart. It is something like a fresh hard-boiled egg lying in front of you; but you don't want to eat it – why, because as if by a prophetic sixth sense you already know that the egg lacks the yoke essential to it - the yoke which makes an egg of it in the first place. So it is natural for such a proposition not to tempt you. This is what perhaps the future seems to those of us who lead such lives.

And this yoke is nothing but the golden glow of love; love that inspires living. Love - that makes life worth its pain. Love - that makes one conserve oneself. The people in this reckless race are the ones who see no real love in their lives; neither in the present nor in the future. They see no reason to preserve or nurture their lives. They are living only for the mad intoxicating moment. It is as if the sun is missing from the lives of such people. They have to put up with cold and damp weather everyday of their existence and the future they perceive has no sun rising there as well.

Sitting behind the wheel - you slowly begin to pick up speed, and then start going faster and faster, and then you come to a sound barrier or a threshold, which once you cross – you suddenly find yourself hurtling into a deep bottomless abyss. The sad part is that you just wouldn't know when exactly you are crossing this threshold; it is only when you find yourself spinning beyond control that you realize the extreme danger.

For attempting a safe exit – the first thing you do is to remove your foot from the gas pedal, and slow down. Give yourself a chance. For a change, put yourself into a safe-lane and cruise slowly at moderate pace. Once you begin to slow down, you will start to notice the small joys catching up with you – in large numbers. The track then bifurcates - the left opening up into a vast green meadow, and the right onto a beach. The only risk you face there - is the risk of realizing that life has only just begun; it is a new you and a new life. The past from there seems like a rotting shipwreck at the bottom of the sea.'

One Deadly Smile

(You know how it is when you desperately want to drink? It was one of those days, when I hit the 'tavern'- the nondescript drinking hole in the east end of town. There I met an old soldier- once an officer in the President's service. He was just about two drinks down, when I took the stool next to him. He asked me for a match to light his cigarette and that is how we got talking. Having not much idea of a soldier's life; pouring him a drink, I asked my companion to recollect some evening from his bygone years in uniform. Slowly taking a sip of the scotch, he revisited an old memory)

'After walking stealthily for about eight hours we finally reached the pre-determined site and settled into a quiet ambush, in a thick grove of walnut trees (this was in South Kashmir, during the peak of insurgency in the state). With bated breaths we waited in the grove, at the edge of this notorious village – ready to pull our frozen fingers on the cold metal triggers if any terrorist walked on the track towards us. That night, the dogs barked and barked - which was a likely indicator for move of terrorists within the village (at that unusual time of the night i.e. one am); but no luck! Though we kept looking at the track unblinkingly through our hand-held thermal imagers, but no one walked into our death trap that night. The terrorists perhaps took a different route out of the village.

As if that was not bad enough, just about the same time, a heavy rain broke out from nowhere. 'Heavy' would be an understatement. It was rather a pouring of water over us. Now two choices lay ahead; either continue sitting in the ambush and getting drenched, or walk seven to eight hours in the rain to get back to our camp. Despite the bloody rain, we waited in ambush for two more hours – in desperation for a kill. Each minute was like an hour and the raindrops only seemed to be growing larger. Water now ran in steady driblets down each man's neck, over his back and into the ground below. By now most men had begun to sneeze. As surprise could no longer be maintained, we finally decided to call off the ambush. Swiftly we moved out, met at the rendezvous, took stock of ourselves and commenced our move back to the camp.

I won't forget that night easily; I couldn't see the track or the road, or even the soldier ahead of me. I had to literally put my hand on the back of the guy ahead to know which way to walk. Everything seemed the darkest possible shade of black. I have lost count as to how many times I slipped and fell into the knee-deep slush of the paddy fields that night (while on our way back). I was in a foul mood, trudging along silently and cursing our futile ambush effort – with clothes completely drenched and water still flowing down our back and legs. Nothing (repeat nothing) was visible – and the goddamn road was still an hour's walk away. After what seemed like eternity, we finally hit the road. I swear I will never forget that one deadly smile! As we hit the road there was this forlorn bulb, which was hanging there in the rain - naked on a bamboo pole, to illuminate a small *'peer baba tomb*[1]' next to it.

Some light from the dim bulb fell on the road, and in that pool of light I hesitated and momentarily halted when I saw an animal's bonny smile lying on the road. It was an old decayed jaw bone - of a cow or a horse, complete with teeth and all; which had been washed and weathered over time to a smooth and gleaming white - and now shone without pity. I heard what this deadly smile had to say, it said "Cheer up old boy! If I still have reason to smile - you fucking well smile as well! Life's not that bad if you are still alive!" And then I confess, I hesitantly smiled a little to myself and then a little more. It came to me in a flash that I was kicking and alive, and on returning to the camp a hot bath and a drink awaited me. And then of course, just a week later I was due to proceed on leave; and at that moment, I dare say – my smile outdid the one lying on the road.'

---

1 An anonymous tomb believed to possess magical powers to help the faithful

Seeking a Job

Ashwin was not really a genius or a bright spark. But what went in his favour was that he was a persevering kind of a fellow - never giving up. This made him finally reach the places where he aimed to get to (even if it took a little more time than his peers who were brighter). His folks were of course proud of him. Today was quite alike to the previous eighteen occasions, when he had appeared for various job interviews in different construction companies – but with no success. Here again he waited, in the reception lounge for his nineteenth job interview. He had been particularly careful today (as previously) in matching his tie, socks and belt with his fawn coloured premium cotton suit. But broadly speaking, it was not Ashwin's habit to be overtly bothered for his appearance. He believed as he had been taught in his childhood, that what was important, were not the clothes but the credentials of the man who wore them. And thus, over a period of time he had steadily built up his academic qualifications. Having completed his Bachelors in Architecture (B Arch) from a reputed college, and with decent grades, Ashwin desperately wanted to join the Drawing and Planning Section of any of the leading construction companies in the country. While he had really prepared hard and tried his best on all previous occasions – there just didn't seem enough vacancies or the right openings to absorb a man of his esteemed qualifications. In between call letters did come for him to join up as teacher, assistant to a surveyor, a lower division bank clerk, agent in the life insurance sector, as a booking officer in the Railways Parcel Office and others – but Ashwin was determined to only take up a planning and designing assignment as per his choice and nothing less. He was thus 'in waiting' for the right opening and disliked being considered jobless; so what if he was waiting for the last four years.

Besides him, there were about forty more aspirants for the same post; and the interviews had been going on for the last three days. Since none of the others seemed interested in talking, Ashwin patiently waited his turn, and to bide away the time - scanned the posters which were on the lounge walls viz. on various ongoing projects of the construction company in different cities, on different grades of cement, benefits of anti-termite treatment of foundations, on the seven keys to success, the definition of happiness and the last of all was a colourful one on the importance of appreciating the beautiful world in which we were blessed to be; and directly under this poster, as if providentially, sat the young and attractive Receptionist - filling up the personal particulars of Ashwin and the other candidates on their interview sheets. She not only was appealing to look at, but had a wonderful texture of voice too; in which she informed Ashwin that he would be the last of the eight candidates in the sequence for today's interviews. In this Ashwin saw the hand of fate, since eight was one of his lucky numbers (along with three, five, eleven, seventeen, twenty three and forty four – as per their family astrologer). Now having time to contemplate and recline on the sofa back, he shifted his focus once more to the receptionist.

She was neither thin nor fat, was adequately tall, a little healthier than athletic (wholesome if you may say) and had long black hair that luxuriantly reached about a hand span below the small of her back. She was dusky of complexion, with full hips and a strapping figure. Not being one of the fragile and tender kinds; she looked sturdy and resilient. May be she was single, available, keen or could be engaged? Such and similar ambitious thoughts raced through Ashwin's fertile mind. Even though being a little hesitant in such matters, he expeditiously harnessed his courage and opened a conversation with the girl. She was quite open to the questions that Ashwin asked her and so the two got on to be talking pretty amicably. Her name was Vaibhavi. She was twenty three years of age and hailed from an orthodox Brahmin family. The conversation between them soon meandered to how difficult it had become to get a decent job these days and how the young had to struggle for an opening.

They both agreed as to how sometimes 'one's qualifications' instead of helping get a job simply came in the way and resulted in so many other wasted opportunities. But Vaibhavi was thankful to *Lord Balaji* (of *Tirupati*) for bestowing upon her this Receptionist's job – which provided sufficiently for her to look after herself in this big city, teeming with unemployed youth (perhaps even better qualified than her).

Vaibhavi offered an analogy – it was like while you went fishing you decided that you would eat only trout;

and no matter how hungry you were, if you caught any salmon, pike, tuna or eel you would simply let them go. Even if it meant going without food for a year or more! (to which both smiled together). Her job as a Receptionist, at the end of the day was a clean job (as she said) - allowing her an air conditioned environment and a five day week. They had a candid exchange of ideas and Ashwin learnt that since Vaibhavi doubled as a Receptionist as well as a Secretary; her job consisted primarily of managing the clients, fixing of appointments, scheduling the boss's weekly and monthly itinerary, sending timely bouquets to his wife, making office memos, taking down dictations, accompanying the boss on site visits (both in and out of the city) and whatever other small or sundry tasks were asked of her. Also she had lately picked up short hand to improve her speed at taking down notes.

And now came Ashwin's turn for the interview. He walked in with a confident stride, faced the panel across the table and answered all their questions - as well as he could (like on all previous interviews). They then asked him about his job experience; since having graduated about four years ago he was yet to make a beginning (this was like touching his raw nerve). And then at the end like always, they said they would let him know (he almost knew what it meant). But then it was already decided that he would neither give up trying nor compromise his job preferences (for lesser options).

Anyway now it was time for him to get back home. While leaving he thought of exchanging telephone numbers with Vaibhavi and following up on their brief association (one never knew the unimaginable possibilities which might unfold in one's future, with a little initiative; and then of course he had heard the stories about all those bold and adventurous office secretaries). Bringing him back to the present, she asked him how his interview had gone; and also added how sure she was that he would finally get the job. Then politely she asked him the subjects with which he had graduated and his qualifications (just for curiosity sake she said). Ashwin promptly and proudly spelt out all his credentials along with mentioning his domain specialization in 'Construction Designing'; and also how he had been 'in- waiting' for the last four years. And then because it seemed only natural, he asked Vaibhavi her qualifications too. At this she smiled and simply replied - that she in the present circumstances had accustomed herself to eating tuna, till she finally caught some trout! But when Ashwin persisted and pressed her with "What exactly have you graduated in?" The beautiful receptionist took a moment and then quite matter-of-factly replied "Sir, I am a Master's of Science in Genetics, from the University of Illinois, USA".

Wild Animals

As Gautam sat in his hotel room he was fully aware of the heavy rain splattering against the window panes. Not because he could hear the splatter but because he saw water flowing down the fogged windows. Being an introvert and a withdrawn person (if one may say), what he liked best about these Five Star hotel suites was the way in which they blocked out all the noise of this ever rushing world. So, Gautam taking occasional short holidays in Five Star hotels (picking the best deals on Group On, Snap Deals, Easy Holidays etc.), carved a silent niche for himself in this crazily spinning world (seeming always to be in the middle of an epileptic fit). Today again (like on all previous occasions) he sat alone, sinking into the deep and overwhelming silence of the hotel suite.

As he peered out into the darkness from the window, he was taken aback to see the gleaming eyes of the hordes of wild animals crawling on the ground down below - eleven stories below to be exact. Two trails of countless animals with their gleaming eyes were going in the opposite directions. Then he realized that there were desperate men sitting in the bellies of each of these monsters. Who drove or controlled the other was a matter of conjecture - whether the man controlled the monster or the monster had a will of its own and simply carried the man, remained unclear. The horses, camels and the elephants of his forefathers times had all been done away with and were replaced by these small and large mechanical species called the 'Automobiles' – which needed no food, but survived only on gas. Gautam for once felt safe and secure in his quiet and silent refuge; lucky not to be in the flow of monsters down below. They never ceased. While the man would die one day, these monsters were immortal; each organ of their body easily renewable.

Gautam suddenly felt tired of all this thinking and speculation; he never seemed to have all the answers anyway. Down below – life in the mad jungle continued. The monsters with their eyes shining bright in the dark – like hyenas – were on the prowl. But Gautam had nothing to fear. No one knew that he was up here on the eleventh floor all by himself – in the cascading silence and the quiet solitude of his hotel suite. Pouring himself yet another martini, he sank once more into the black leather sofa next to the window, and saw the heavy rain running quietly down the glass panes.

The Scent of Mangoes

She sells the sweet smelling alphonso mangoes next to the stinky drain behind the maternity hospital. It's been so long that she doesn't feel the suffocating stink from the drain anymore. Being the only vendor selling alphonso mangoes at the drain, makes it easier for her customers to spot her and gives her an easy publicity. Moreover being close to the maternity hospital gets her sufficient customers as well. She herself has never liked the taste of alphonsos; so she can't understand why they are such a rage. One reason may be that she herself has eaten only those which are far over-ripe or a little rotten (and the ones which do not sell). She as a matter of fact has a very poor appetite and seldom eats. How people can possibly have three meals a day is beyond her understanding. Her stomach since birth is conditioned to only one or at best two small meals a day. She has long forgotten her age and doesn't really care much for it. If asked to make a guess, she says she maybe ninety plus. Her parents had died of cholera when she was only a child, leaving her to be brought up in an orphanage. Then for a very long time, she worked as a daily labour at different road construction sites; till she had contracted tuberculosis, with the dense smoke of burning tar clogging her lungs. And though she did marry; her husband after a few years had run away with another woman from the neighbouring village. She doesn't know where he is now (or even if he is dead or alive). Children - she never had from her marriage. It is selling mangoes since as long as she can recollect that she has been able to provide for herself. She has no savings for a rainy day; and in case it pours, she is ready to be washed away. In her recent pilgrimage to *Tirupati Balaji* (the shrine of *Lord Venkateswara* - located atop the Tirumala Hills in Southern India) she donated all that she had put together in the last ten years. She believes that having donated it all, will absolve her of all her sins (if any) ever committed by her unknowingly. Meanwhile she takes life one day at a time and future plans - she has none. All her old friends are by and by gone. With her spirits waning, she knows that her time too is soon approaching. However it least disturbs her. The only step she has taken is to have kept an advance of a hundred rupees with the caretaker of the local crematorium, to pay for her final expenses (whenever that is). Till then she continues selling mangoes behind the maternity hospital, near the stinky drain as usual.

The Goal

Ginny's parents were tough mountain goats, and they were initially quite delighted when Ginny was born; healthy and plump (in fact overweight in comparison to her siblings). However, their excitement soon wore off, when Ginny continued to stay that way. Traditionally, mountain goats were supposed to be lean and thin, just like they themselves were. Ginny however was fat, delicate and always catching a cold. Her parents and brothers in comparison were very strong and tough. Whenever Ginny tried to climb a mountain with her brothers or parents she would tire out very soon. Sometimes she would have severe pain in her legs or would sprain an ankle. Initially it was alright and Ginny felt happy and comfortable with her family; but soon they started making fun of her and ridiculing her. They also started calling her names, such as weakling, sissy, fatso and so on. Ginny felt terrible, and while others slept during the night, she would cry silently – feeling humiliated and helpless.

However, one thing which no one knew was that within the soft and weak appearing Ginny was the toughest mountain goat ever born. She soon got over her desperation, strengthened her inner core and finally decided to take the situation into her own hands. Though no one had any expectations from Ginny and considered her most useless and weak, Ginny was no more perturbed because she knew in her heart what she was capable of. So one fine day Ginny decided it was time she started preparing herself for a challenge – something to prove her grit and determination. Though she was alone in her resolve but she never lost faith in herself.

Ginny silently began to work on herself. She started with eating less and exercising more. While everyone slept, Ginny would stay awake at nights - thinking of a befitting challenge for herself. One of these nights, she heard the old goats talk about a mountain called 'Heaven Snow' - which no goat had ever been able to scale as yet. It was said by the old goats that 'Heaven Snow' could never be climbed and that several goats had been defeated by its icy winds and snow covered slopes. Even Ginny's father, who took great pride in his strength, had failed thrice in the peak of his youth to climb 'Heaven Snow'.

Ginny had now found her challenge; she decided to climb 'Heaven Snow', no matter what the odds. However, she did not share her ambition with anyone, lest they laugh and make fun of her. There was only one person in the world with whom Ginny could share her dream and that was her Grandpa. He loved her very dearly. So the next morning Ginny set out to meet her Grandpa, who lived in a deep forest all by himself. Her Grandpa was absolutely delighted to see her and gave Ginny a warm hug. Then her Grandpa said to her, "Ginny my child, why don't you tell me your plans? I can see it in your eyes that you are here today to share something very special with me? Come on

Ginny, I am anxious to know the secret which has brought you here today?"

And then for the first time, sharing her secret, Ginny with eyes shining brightly and voice full of confidence said, "Grandpa I have decided to climb 'Heaven Snow', and I am here today to seek your blessings".

Grandpa's eyes were full of tears and he said to Ginny, "My dear Ginny, the day you were born I knew you were special and that one day you would achieve what no one has ever achieved before". Then Grandpa also said to Ginny, "Ginny, my love and blessings are with you, and while 'Heaven Snow' waits for you to begin climbing – remember that 'Heaven Snow' is a very steep mountain with strong blizzards around it. But come what may, I want you to never forget your dream. Whenever you find yourself losing strength, just remember your goal". He further said, "Ginny, my tough child, there is no time to waste, you must start climbing soon - because the season for snow storms is fast approaching, which could make your climb even more difficult".

So, the next morning Ginny hugged her Grandpa, took his blessing and said a silent prayer to her God. Then she looked up at 'Heaven Snow' and said, "Heaven Snow, you may be a tough mountain but I am also a tough mountain goat and very soon we will meet at the summit". Slowly and steadily Ginny began the climb. She kept climbing the whole day and the whole night. Initially everyone thought that Ginny was away for a vacation at her Grandpa's house, but very soon the word of her daring attempt spread through the whole village. Ginny's father commented, "Stupid Ginny, she is going to kill herself", and her brothers made jokes about her being fat and weak. The whole village was scared that Ginny would die.

In the course of the long climb, Ginny became exhausted and was quite cold. She even had severe muscle cramps and fever, but then - she was not just another goat and kept on climbing. During her climb it rained heavily and icy winds blew in her face, but Ginny never lost sight of her goal and persisted with the climb - slowly and steadily. Ginny also recollected that her Grandpa had called her 'Special'; this gave her strength and she continued one step at a time. Ginny had never climbed to such a height before and she now had problems in breathing, but then she was not going to lose this battle so easily. This was not just about climbing a mountain, but about proving something to herself. She kept on climbing and by the end of the sixth day, Ginny had become rather weak and thin. On the seventh day, when her energy was waning and her spirits were really low, she still managed to lift her head and shout, "Heaven Snow, don't try to scare me, I am certainly going to be on top – no matter how hard you try to turn me back".

Finally on the eighth day, Ginny could see the summit in the distance. It was still about seven to eight hours away. But now the snow had turned to ice and was very slippery and hard. After each step that she took, she would slip two steps back. Ginny's progress had come to a total halt and she now realized that it was not for nothing, that 'Heaven Snow' was known as the most difficult mountain and had taken so many lives.

An idea suddenly came to Ginny. First with her horns she dug some snow and then placed her foot, and again she dug some more snow and took the next step. This way she did not slip. Though, painfully laborious and slow, but she in this manner kept inching towards the summit. Finally came this golden moment, when Ginny realized her dream – As she took in a breath and climbed a little more; she felt a very strong gust of wind and suddenly there was no more mountain left to climb. As she looked around, she saw only the skies. The clouds were below her. She, once upon a time 'fatso and weakling' had made it to the summit; 'Heaven Snow' was silent and humble beneath her feet. Ginny stood taller than any other mountain goat in the world, and her village appeared to be barely a speck of dust from where she stood.

Ginny had conquered 'Heaven Snow', and as she stood in that moment, she heard a deep voice, "Hello! Ginny, I am Heaven Snow. I want to tell you that you are the toughest goat I've ever seen, and I am honoured that today we meet at the summit. I will always remember your courage and strength". While Ginny stood at the top of 'Heaven Snow', the weather all of a sudden cleared. The clouds disappeared, the rain stopped and the sun began to shine more brightly then it had ever shone before. Someone from her village down below yelled, "Hey everybody, look at the top of 'Heaven Snow'. There appears to be a goat up there, look carefully". And everyone said, "Yes, yes we can see there is a goat standing on top of 'Heaven Snow'. Who the hell can it be? Or is it just a dream?"

Then, Grandpa who had kept quiet all this while, shouted, "You stupid fools, the goat you see up there is not a dream. It is none other than our very own Ginny, the 'toughest mountain goat' ever born; the first one ever to climb 'Heaven Snow' in a thousand years. Let us all say, Long Live Ginny". It was a little strange, but in this moment of glory while they should have rejoiced – Ginny's father, mother and brothers were all sullen and dumb. They appeared to be ashamed of themselves and suddenly inflicted with an unknown sorrow. Anyway no one had much time to notice them anymore.

Finally, when Ginny climbed down the 'Heaven Snow' and reached her village, her Grandpa was the first to receive her with tears of joy in his eyes. And as he hugged her tight, he said, "Ginny my child, I am proud of you – just like always". This brought tears of joy to Ginny too and washed away all her pain, accumulated over the years.

That night Grandpa arranged a grand celebration in honour of Ginny. Every goat from villages near and far came to see 'Ginny – The Conqueror of Heaven Snow'. That is how she was known always ever after.

Late in the night, when the party ended and as almost everyone had left – one small goat with a deformed leg, limped out of the dark shadows towards Ginny. His voice was feeble and his head hung low; his self-esteem appeared to have been stolen and it seemed as if he was ashamed of his existence. But then, despite all this, the feeble and lame goat told Ginny that he too wanted to attempt something significant like she had done; and how he felt inspired by her. This brought back some old and familiar memories to Ginny. She smiled and said to the young goat, "Don't bother about what other people think of you, and don't let them fix your place in life. You and you alone can set your goals, because only you know who you are."

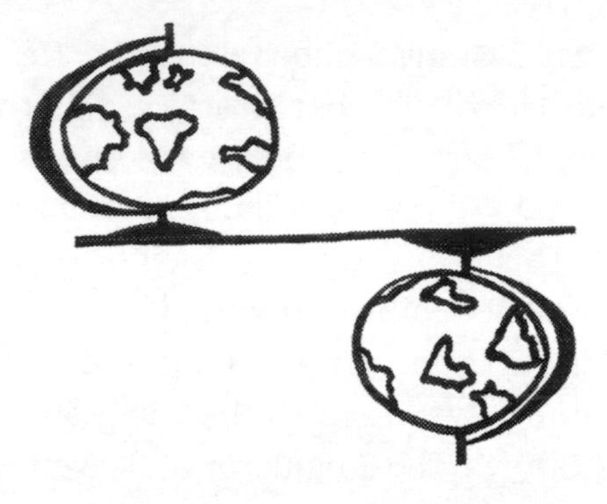

The Two Worlds

(From the notes of a man who often passed-by a graveyard, on his way to work)

'Passing by graveyards and cemeteries has always affected my disposition. I have on such occasions become noticeably calm, somber and introspective. I have seen graveyards withstand heavy rains, snow and sleet, without the residents ever rushing for umbrellas or cover. And then, I have seen them braving the tormenting Indian summer, without ever a grudge for lack of air conditioning. Being a neutral observer, I have often wondered how the weather fails to impinge on our neighbors. They, I think in the true sense of the word, are the ultimate survivors - more resilient and more hardened against the petty stuff that bugs us all our life.

I wonder if there are two worlds that exist together - one, the Up Above and the other, the Down Under; each of them a sovereign nation, and self-sufficient in itself.

The world me and you exist in today, is of course, the Up Above world. And sooner or later, most of us (because there are some amongst us, of whom one can never be sure!) will quietly or may be noisily, transition into the Down Under world. Just as when you travel from one country to another, you have to pass through airports, immigration offices, border check posts etc; similarly, there are transition points, from where you either slowly, swiftly or very suddenly transit from the Up Above to the Down Under. More popular amongst these crossing places are multi-facility hospitals, fully equipped trauma care centers, cars and scooters travelling at high speeds, railway lines etc. Some less popular places are of course the balconies of high-rise buildings, ceiling fans, animal safaris, bars hosting mafia parties, schools and banks. The list of places from where one can transition is in fact rather long.

I wonder who the better of us both is - we, the citizens of the Up Above, or they, the denizens of the Down Under. Till we arrange a symposium between both houses, I would like to believe that it is perhaps equally tricky in both places. Like those of us staying and working in the city - yearn to be in the hills; while those living in the hills - want to move to the city. So I guess that is how it is with the folk on either side. Those tired of living - don't die, and those sick of being dead - don't come to life again.

Do they exist in greater peace than us? Not having to deal with mean bosses, tight parking places, filing tax returns, diabetes etc.? I wonder if they have a currency of their own. And what about their government, is it elected or a monarchy? Or do they have a home grown Hitler? How is the state of inflation down under? What kind of stuff do they shop for? (Not to forget that there are some very fashionable and page 3 type of people down there too). Do they sell frozen stuff and exotic fruits down there? Do they have their share of strikes, demonstrations and riots? Whatever it may be, one thing is sure, they don't have much time for us. Theirs is a busy life. They don't have the leisure or the inclination to deal with living people like us on a regular basis.

Surprisingly though, with such large populations on either side, both our worlds appear seemingly in peace and perfect harmony with each other. You never hear of boundary disputes, patrol clashes or land encroachments amongst the neighbors. Sometimes (though rarely) border violations do get reported by the folk Up Above. Some from the Up Above, have at times alleged, an odd citizen or two from the Down Under sneaking around in white clothes during the night - often with a missing head, missing limbs, or with disfigured faces. And once having been encountered, they have always vanished into thin air.

Not having to be burnt or buried as yet, I have often felt gratitude to be a citizen of the Up Above. That is gratitude for still being alive and enjoying the distractions and indulgences of this illusionary world! (which according to spiritual masters is simply *Bhram*[2]). On occasions when I have been stressed (which I am most often, except for brief periods when I am in the loo), I have envied the guys Down Under. They seem to be in bliss and living a hassle free life (just as the tomb stones say – 'here rests in peace'). Then I wonder, maybe it is not true; maybe it is something I just want to believe (you know our donkey sense of finding grass to be always greener on the other side). May be the folk down below too have their own indigenous privations, anxieties and trepidations?

---

[2] Just a figment of our imagination (in Hindi)

It may be only a matter of time and concerted dialogue that tourist visas soon come into force between both nations. Just as we have explored space and discovered the secrets of the sea, may be the residents of either world, in future, will visit and discover each other. But by then, I am likely to have moved on and acquired the nationality of the Down Under.

As you drive or dive, or burrow past, and call upon your resting neighbors, it would be easier recognizing me if you remember that I have three artificial teeth, a steel rod in my right forearm and a very broad forehead (which according to my children can solve the parking problems of a metro as large as Delhi).'

Buying a Bentley

When the Bentley came out in a Cobalt Blue color and with design changes that immediately appealed to his heart, Petrios knew that this was the car he had long been waiting for. Driving his Volkswagen pick-up had though become a habit of years - it was now time to change old habits. It was an added excitement that no one as yet had driven around in a Cobalt Blue Bentley in this part of Ohio. When you are young and not yet into the deep forest of middle age, acquiring a new car makes your hormones spurt stronger and opens new vistas of exciting possibilities to rev up your personal life as well. Sometimes small things impact people differently; for example boys when they see a face and happen to like it, nothing else matters. But with girls they measured you well - taking into account every little detail of your life. Like which part of the town you lived, the kind of house you stayed, the dog you walked, the clothes you wore, the cologne you sported and of course the car you stepped out from.

Taking a quick shower followed by black coffee along with bacon and eggs was how he started his day. Sometimes he would head straight to his office downtown or at times his boss would call him up with a list of prospective clients to whom Petrios that day would try and sell the various insurance plans the company had in its kitty. But this morning he had more important business and had already taken the day off. The cheque book was sitting safely in his breast pocket as he turned on the ignition of his faithful Volkswagen yet another time. This car reminded him of one of his old uncles who just refused to die or even as to fall ill (until he was disowned by the family). Looking the time in his watch, Petrios guessed that in the next about forty minutes he would be at the Bentley Showroom collecting the keys to his new car. Just the thought of it made his pulse to race.

Shifting into the fifth gear and cruising along the straight road, Petrios saw the last couple of years replaying themselves in his rear view mirror. Having separated from his wife - had allowed him an unforeseen run on the highway once more. Three girl friends had come and gone like petrol stations passing by in quick succession. But now was a dry patch that he was going through. Although he had been working on Sandra for about a year now, but you know how some fish take all the time in the world and still hesitate to bite? Sandra was like that - she headed the Home Loans section in the same office. And the very first time that he had seen her, he had noted as to how beautifully her lips curled and eyes twinkled whenever she smiled at you. Of course there was much more to Sandra than just her lips and twinkling eyes which enamored Petrios. Sandra was unlike other girls; who whenever they wanted to freak out just let their hair down. Instead, Sandra's far focus on a comfortable and secure life kept her well away from any mindless adventures. She incidentally attached great importance to the car anyone drove around. Naturally if anyone splurged on a fancy car, it meant he had sufficient bootie for other stuff too. So Petrios concluded that if he could serve up this ace he might lift the Grand Slam this time.

Having arrived he pulled his Volkswagen neatly into the parking and walked up to the showroom. The salesperson greeted him with the customary warmth and put him in touch with the store manager; with whom he had worked out the details of the deal in advance. The papers having already been prepared, Petrios quickly signed over the dotted line and wrote out the cheque for his new car. The vehicle in the next few minutes was prepared for delivery – ribbons tied and rosebuds neatly stuck to the bonnet etc. The keys felt nice and heavy in Petrios's palm. With five litres of petrol having been provided by the showroom the Bentley stood ready to be driven out. The engine purred with promise and the car sailed smoothly on the black asphalt river. Driving home, Petrios smiled at all the adulation which a new car draws. The rest of the day passed-by in anticipation of good things to follow.

Petrios was early at the office the next day, so that his Bentley could be sitting up in the car park all alone - and be noticed by one and all as they arrived. As the day started the buzz slowly got around, as to 'Whose new car was it?' though the question hadn't quite directly reached Petrios as yet. Sandra today wore a crisp yellow frock with small white daisies (or were they geraniums?) on it. The frock finished a little above her knees and made her look like a tender bud herself. Her hair was open and the fragrance of the peach shampoo slowly permeated the whole office (which Petrios so loved). Breezing past Petrios to the Boss's office, she suddenly halted and turned towards him with a "Hey! Petrios, you notice the blue baby in the crèche today?" Petrios, keeping his breathing normal answered back quite matter-of-factly "Of Course! You like it?" Sandra replied "Like it? You gotta be kidding. I'd die just to drive it once!" And Petrios slowly pulled out the gleaming car keys and stretched his hand out to Sandra saying "Here, go ahead!" Sandra jumped and "Don't tell me! You bought it!" was followed by "Oh! What a color. My favorite you know!" (Who else would, if Petrios didn't?).

And then the next day being Easter it was decided that Sandra was driving out into the country with Petrios - for the full day. Sleep eluded Petrios that night. He woke up early; packing an ice bucket and two bottles of Sandra's favorite cherry wine into the boot space. He put in other important stuff too - whatever in his wisdom Sandra could possibly need in the country side. And most importantly, he prepared himself to make progress with Sandra today. It was a bright morning with a mild westerly breeze and seemingly just the right climate to get the fish to bite. Driving up to Sandra's apartment Petrios waited below. Coming out and walking over, Sandra looked like a scandal - in tight denim shorts and a sheer pink Arizona baseball tee shirt. Her skin reflected smooth like marble and her hair glistened like the finest dark silk ever. Petrios swallowed and held the door wide open. He could feel a promise unknot itself deep within.

Sandra appreciated the car and seemed to like it very much. The smell of her peach shampoo at close was intoxicating and Petrios checked himself from being distracted. Bringing his mind back to essentials; the first thing he reckoned he needed - was a fill-up. Since the initial five litres of petrol wouldn't be lasting much; he pulled into the first gas station along the highway. Queuing up to the filling line he noticed Trevor behind him (on his bike). Given any usual day Petrios would like to shoot Trevor. The bastard had shamelessly been hitting on Sandra a long time now. Sandra however didn't really like him much – he went around on his old motorcycle (with smoky fumes) and there was no prosperity about the man. But just because he persisted, it had been a kind of neck to neck between him and Trevor for the last almost one year. Today luckily the leech wouldn't be disturbing them. He had not the faintest idea as to who was in the shining Bentley ahead of him and thankfully Sandra hadn't noticed the bugger either. They would fill-up and shoot into the future before Trevor realized his luck passing. The car ahead moved on and it was now Petrios's turn. Even with his attention divided in three places (i.e. towards watching the gas filling meter, keeping an eye on the asshole behind and making unsuspecting conversation with Sandra going) he stylishly eased the Bentley astride the curbside pump. Handing over his credit card to the sales person he asked him for his usual fill-up of the tank. The capacity being forty litres it took a while to top-up; with the ass behind still sitting patiently on his bike (unaware of how life was passing him by) and Sandra excitedly telling Petrios of how her pet canaries had for the first time eaten straight out of her hands this morning.

The tank topped-up, the sales person swiped the card and brought back the receipt for Petrios's signature. Giving the sales boy a generous tip, he turned towards Sandra to see her check her lipstick in the mirror. Having finished talking of her canaries, she was now apparently telling him about a St. Bernard which she once had as a kid. And who was obsessed with eating their neighbor's petunias. Petrios smiled and agreed vehemently with whatever she was saying. The tank having been filled-up, they were now ready to start measuring the roads in Ohio City; while Trevor waited behind for them to move on - so that he could refuel his bike too.

But then Trevor waited and waited and waited still more – as the Bentley's engine just didn't fire. The car only spluttered and shook and fumed like an old suffering patient of whooping cough; only it didn't move an inch. Something was terribly wrong. While Petrios flogged the dead horse; the smoke and the heavy fumes had found their way into the Bentley and Sandra already was coughing deliriously and incessant tears rolled from her eyes. What a rotten piece of luck! (Cursed Petrios) that the machine had to give up here and now (at this tender life changing moment). What possibly could have gone wrong with such an excessively new car? Amused by the drama the staff at the gas station and a bunch of customers had already gathered around the unyielding Bentley. And then it suddenly clicked to Petrios (like all the six sides of a rubix cube coming together) – that while ordering the refueling he had fallen prey to the old habit of his Volkswagen - and had ordered for a 'Diesel' top-up in his new 'Petrol run !' Bentley.

He wanted to cry and howl and wail loudly and beat his chest – but given the audience, Petrios couldn't do it. Sandra meantime, almost fainting with asphyxia had tumbled out – and stood gasping for fresh air. How Petrios swore (which in words would be indecent to reproduce) and wished he hadn't blundered; was a pitiful site to see. But worse was yet to come. The leech of a guy - Trevor, noticing Sandra, had crept up to her and now had his rotten arm around her dainty shoulders; and dabbed her doe like eyes with his goddamn handkerchief. Disgustingly - Sandra too was leaning on him as if she had been poisoned to death. And then understanding the nature of the calamity - Trevor burst out into a loud fit of laughter (which according to Petrios could have been heard up to five miles around) along with repetitively slapping Petrios's back (in uncontrolled ecstasy). Petrios further reeled with horror when he saw that Trevor's old bullock cart of a bike was missing from under his ass; and now what he sat upon was a brand new 1000 cc Harley Davidson. Lifting Sandra from the waist he put her on the pillion and then after filling-up (the right fuel!) in his bike rode away into the countryside. The last time Petrios saw Sandra was when she said 'Sorry!' and clasped Trevor tightly around his waist, as they drove out of the gas station that Easter afternoon.

The engine having ceased, the Bentley subsequently had to be weighed and sold off as scrap, at a junk yard. Petrios still going single has gone back to driving his old Volkswagen and is currently seeking treatment for his everlasting deep phobia of all gas stations!

An Old Story

This story is of long long ago, of the olden days; of the days when mysterious and un-believable things happened on our planet. And it goes that there was then a unique breed of Giants; who were astoundingly big and tall and very strong. They said their bodies were not of mortal flesh, but of iron and that they were imperishable and invincible.

When man came out of his caves and started settling down his towns and villages; the giants didn't fight his plans, but being of humble temperament – they simply gave man the right of way. And as for themselves, they quietly moved out into the countryside. For years no one saw them or heard of them or knew where they slept or what they ate. But just because they were so big and somewhere out there in the wilderness – man couldn't sleep in peace and suspected that one fine day they might come back and threaten his existence. But then there was nothing he could do about it; the giants simply being too big and too strong for him. He tried very hard to kill them but his arrows, spears and maces were of no avail. Then one day man thought about this with his brothers. They had to find a solution. How long could they live in such an atmosphere of suspense. And just because there was no way they could be killed, man planned to trap and tie up these giants.

So at night he laid his vicious traps in the countryside. And the giants, unsuspecting, were snared and caught in the course of their innocent wandering. Once caught, they were tightly tied up by man. While the giants didn't resist; man still continued to tighten his ropes every morning and night. Till one day the ropes cut into the giants. And their blood flowed. This blood ran into the ropes and was carried and reached the habitations of man.

And then a miracle happened. The blood of the giants - wherever it reached, it burst into brightness; the brightness of a kind that had never been seen before. They said that darkness died that day. Even today if you drive up into the countryside, you can still see the giants standing there silently - all tied-up and trapped; and their blood still running through the ropes.

While man continuing to wonder as to who these giants were, how they came to be or who sent them here; hasn't yet the time to listen - to what the old and wizened eagle has to say. The same old eagle, who they say never dies and flies beyond the skies. It says "these are the children of the Sun God - sent here by their father to destroy 'darkness', his old enemy". But the man only laughs and calls them the 'Pylons'.

Woman

(Exclusively penned for Khushboo, my daughter)

(Going through other people's personal diaries (when they aren't looking) is neither politically nor morally right, but one summer I happened to be doing just that. It was perhaps the diary of a daughter's father (with a lot of little entries about the relationship which is so sweet). It almost drew my tears. But one little note, which the man had penned for his daughter was really interesting and I couldn't stop from pulling out the leaf and putting it away into my pocket. Let me just unfold it here and allow you a reading, perhaps you too are a daughter's father like me)

'Just as God made man, so he made woman. They are both equal in their rights and privileges when born, but it is by virtue of the male dominance in our society that men have positioned themselves a step higher and have labeled the female sex with the all too common clichés such as, the weaker sex, the burden on the family, someone who will leave the family one day, someone who needs protection, someone more prone to exploitation, someone less intelligent, the more talkative breed etc.

It is undoubtedly true that most males of this world (myself being one), let us call them the 'stags', live under a sad illusion that they are perhaps a superior race. This self-belief of theirs is however slowly crumbling and creating complex psychological problems in the poor males of this society. Let us once and for all set our perceptions right, by understanding, with a pinch of salt perhaps - that this is a 'Women's World'. Just as it has always been and shall continue to be. Which unfortunately, the stags with their small brains and large egos have never been able to accept.

You just have to look around or dig a little into history, to realize that there are scores of women who have proven to be path-finders in their chosen fields and torch bearers for this dim world of ours. They have set an example for the entire women race (personally - I prefer to call them the 'superior race', the 'fairer sex', and once married – the 'better halves') to emulate and draw an inspiration. The modern day women with their tact and kick-ass attitude have bounced the scheming males all over the place and have risen to the ultimate pinnacles of power. Women today are Prime Ministers, Presidents, Scientists, Doctors, Designers, Entrepreneurs and what not in our modern world. There is no such thing anymore as an 'exclusive male territory'.

Women today are dictating terms to men. They are the cream of this society; may it be in the field of politics, art, literature or science. But being a stag myself, I humbly confess that for a greater part of my life I too was suffering from the endemic male myopia which doesn't allow one to see all this. It was marriage in my case which finally made me see and accept (of course with an obituary for my poor male ego), that women are definitely sharper, have better memories, greater qualities of man- management, leadership, tact, diplomacy, social attributes, possess better human understanding, are less-selfish, more accommodating, more adjusting, more caring and concerned for their families, better dedicated to their professions and at the same time – the least egoistic about it all. They are better at balancing jobs and family and more dedicated towards them both. They not only have a greater capacity to love but also to forgive. The list would be endless if we went on counting; but for the sake of men, we must stop; because the point has been made and there is no use flogging a dead horse (more so, at the end of the day, I still have to go to and hang out with the men in the bar).

The 'biggest threat' to any male in this world (which no male will ever confess to a woman) is a 'female' who knows that not only is she not inferior to him but instead a step above. Such women make men feel like eunuchs – weak and inferior; and give the stags an acute inferiority complex. So as a woman, a woman has to feel confident and strong, and never let self-doubt or propaganda from the male managed rumour mills cloud her mind or bog her down. Remember the saying – 'someone can climb on to your back only if you bend'. So, it is entirely up to each woman to not allow anyone to ever dominate her or dare even in a dream to exploit or take advantage of her.

So listen woman, no one can ever push you, exploit you or treat you with disrespect or like junk, unless you give the other person space enough to draw an impression that he can dare do so and get away with it. It is entirely in your hands to prevent such impressions taking root in the minds of those meek men around you. The best way I guess is to begin with respecting your own self and enhancing your self- esteem - by understanding your capabilities, having resolute confidence in yourself and listening to your inner voice. Have the strength to believe in your opinions, stick your ground and loudly announce the reasons for your likes and dislikes.

There is nothing to be afraid of in this world. Nothing at all; except your own doubts about yourself. Amongst what is required, is faith in yourself, courage to speak your mind, ability to kick-ass when needed and to live life on your own terms, no matter what the odds. So my dear, the motto of the story (because all stories must have mottos) is to pursue your dreams and live without fear. Remember you are running a race which is already fixed in your favour. The only worthwhile thing left to do is to improve your own timing.'

Burdens We Carry

(He watched a lot of television. And after all there's an awfully attractive and wonderful world inside that little box. One doesn't have to go around the world anymore or sail the high seas; simply switch-on your television and there you are, amongst the sharks in the Atlantic, or shaking a leg with the super stars. And when I asked this man, if lately he had watched anything interesting, this is what he said)

'One day while surfing channels on the television I paused when I saw an interesting documentary - covering different aspects of life in rural India. It reflected on the plight of tribal women in *Bastar*[3]; who eke out a meager living collecting and selling firewood each day. They would first tediously pick-up firewood from the forest for several hours, tie it into bundles, hoist them on their heads and then walk for about fifteen to twenty miles in the sweltering

---

[3] A province in Central India

heat, barefoot to the nearest "*Haat*[4]"; where - selling the wood at bargain prices they would earn as much as about thirty rupees by the end of the day. Generally out of these fifteen to twenty rupees went towards buying coarse rice and some vegetable or cheap fish (if their children had demanded so and if the income that day permitted the luxury). About ten rupees they would hand over to their husbands (generally unemployed or maybe working as casual labour somewhere on daily wages) for buying their daily requirement of '*beedis*[5]' and '*toddy*[6]'. If they were lucky, they saved four to five rupees for a medicine or a *puja*[7] or a festival.

It touched my heart to see these women walk such long distances, barefoot in the sweltering heat every day with their burdens on their heads. And then, as I thought of their burdens which they finally get a price for in the 'Haats', I wondered why no documentary ever gets made on the kinds of burden people carry in the busy cosmopolitan towns. That is the burdens carried by the city folk – people like me and you and so many of us. The burdens that we have been carrying for long years viz. the burdens of not having been loved enough by our parents, burdens of an inferiority complex, burdens of not having done well in our lives, burdens of cheating on our partners, of having doubted our loved ones, of having been too harsh with our kids etc. And just because these burdens are not on our heads, they cannot be seen by a lens or a naked eye; but

---

4 Village market

5 Locally made hand- rolled cigarettes

6 Country liquor

7 Ritual

they are really heavy, even more so than the burdens of the women in Bastar.

We carry these burdens within and we not only carry them for a couple of miles like the women in the village, but for all our lives. Though acquired in our childhood, youth or adolescence; they can never be put down and unlike the burdens of Bastar - cannot be sold at bargain prices in any village market.'

Wonder Why...

1. Wives think they are weak.
2. Husbands think they are strong.
3. Parents think the children are foolish.
4. Children think their secrets are hidden from their parents.
5. While driving our cars we speak of the ever increasing traffic.
6. We worry about the increasing population but hate wearing condoms.
7. While enjoying cigarettes we think of giving up smoking.
8. When a man getting out of a BMW has holes in his jeans - he is rich.

9. When a man riding a bicycle has holes in his jeans - he is poor.

10. The industrialists worry much about disappearing forests.

11. While sex before marriage is a norm, we still expect virgins for our first night.

12. Men want to last longer while women want to get it over quickly.

13. Silicon is now less in the earth and more in the breasts.

14. Drinking is no more to do with milk.

15. What earlier meant natural is now 'organic'.

16. Chemistry amongst young students is no more only a subject.

17. Parents are no more parents, but just friends.

18. Endangered species now includes 'servants'.

19. The only proof of one's existence is now the facebook.

20. Tea turns out perfect only when you make it yourself.

21. The funniest joke is the one your boss cracks.

22. Being stressed is normal and feeling happy - unusual.

23. Our neighbors are always smarter and better-off than us.

A Matter of Honour

Karnail Singh was a fine soldier, a strapping youth – six feet three inches tall (and then three inches more, if you considered his height with his well starched and crisp turban on his head). He was broad chested, with a coiled moustache, a heavy beard (tightly pressed and set with pomade to stay matted on his cheeks). His forearms were thick and covered with dense hair, like coiled wires. He had a booming voice and a laughter that seemed to be coming up in a very broad pipe – straight from his belly. The pupils of his eyes were a bright white and when he looked up at you, it was a piercing look - one that quickly measured you up.

Even the Corporals and the Sergeants quietly acknowledged his strength and refrained from giving him any un-soldierly fatigues, that is, say chopping vegetables or kneading the dough etc. were tasks never assigned to Karnail Singh. Once assigned the task of washing the large cooking utensils, he had simply not turned-up in the company cook house the whole day. And the next morning, putting on his best uniform had reported, unasked, to the Company Sergeant Major to seek punishment for his dereliction of duty. Then he cheerfully ran the twenty kilometers with full battle load (with the best record timing ever in the company) – the punishment awarded to him for neglect of an assigned task.

If it was just one word which you had to choose to describe the man, the word for Karnail Singh was 'proud'. It was not to be confused with haughtiness or arrogance; it was a kind of self-esteem, if I may say which comes with scrupulous upbringing and the honest living of one's past generations. Going back a little into his childhood - it was a bright day and Karnail was only a boy, when a neighbor took him by the ear to his grandfather (called 'Bauji'); complaining that he had caught him red handed, stealing mangoes from his orchard.

When Bauji looked enquiringly at the young Karnail, Karnail simply put his head down (and stared at his old leather sandals). Karnail never forgot his Grandfather apologizing with folded hands to the neighbor, on his behalf that day; and then later telling him affectionately, that "Don't ever do anything that can bring you to shame; for being without a head is better than having one which hangs low".

For Karnail, his Bauji was everything. It was Bauji who had single handedly brought him up - giving him the affection of both a father and a mother; since Karnail's own father had left his mother, when he was just three, to marry another girl from the neighbouring village. And then within a year, his mother too had fallen prey to cholera and withered away in front of his eyes - leaving him, a lad of five years, whose child-hood had come to an abrupt end. It was then that he took up working in his Bauji's fields. It tired him out really well and so that when he would lie down to sleep at night, the voices in his head couldn't make themselves heard. Two years he worked in the field. His hands had become so calloused and rough, that once in a fight he had knocked out a boy – three years his elder and that with a single blow.

Bauji was a man of the old stock and he knew that much before medicine came (which today sold like chick-peas), it was the earth that healed; let a man till the land, or remove the weeds or sow the paddy or harvest a crop and it cured him of his melancholy. So, Bauji let Karnail be by himself and allowed him two years of tilling the land. Then one day he roused him up early from the bed, washed him with soap and much against his wishes put him into a crisp new school uniform. And then putting a satchel on his shoulders, led him by the hand to the village school. There he told the old headmaster (a childhood friend of his) that "I want this boy to become a soldier, a very brave soldier. And so from today, he is not Pritpal (Karnail's old name) but 'Karnail' (the colloquial for a 'Colonel')"; and that his how his name was entered in the school records and so came to be. And years later, as his Bauji had wanted, Karnail enlisted himself in the army.

Whenever a ceremonial guard had to be presented to a visiting general, or if it was an inter-company wrestling contest or a cross-country race or a marathon, that had to be won, or an impression made; Karnail was the first choice on which the roulette stopped. Once in the deserts, when the Company Commander's jeep was stuck in the sand, and seemed to be sinking-in only deeper; Karnail - all alone - had simply lifted it up and put it back on the track - with the Company Commander and the driver still sitting in the vehicle with a dazed look. And then during the drill practices, the heavy 303 (bolt action) spring field rifle, looked like a piece of blighted sugarcane being bounced up by Karnail. Such was the strength in his arms.

When the Battalion had its centenary celebrations, it was a big affair – comprising several ceremonial functions, grand lunches, dinners, entertainment shows and all of it lasting well over three days. The parents and relatives of all the men had been invited to join-in in the gala event. Amongst the guests, were five tall men who attended from Karnail's Village – his Grandfather, the school head master and three more elders from the Village *Panchayat*[8], all well into their late eighties. The stock of Karnail clearly stood out – all over six feet tall, barrel chested, proud, with big moustaches, heavy beards and booming voices. They all wore their spotless white *kurta-pajamas*[9] and large starched *pagris*[10] on their heads. One more commonality which they had and clearly stood out – was their unanimous joy and pride in seeing Karnail in his olive green uniform.

During the introduction with the Company Commander, they pressed the Company Commander's hand so hard (in their natural exuberance) – that the poor man winced; and became wiser to only greet them with folded hands thereafter. The three days went by like a breeze and now it was the time for farewells. The Company Commander at the see-off couldn't hold back from telling Karnail's grandfather – as to what a pleasure it was to him to have a man such as Karnail in his outfit. The Grandfather listened in the manner of a man – used to hearing this all the time; and then asked of the Company Commander only one thing – that whenever the time came, in the face of the enemy, to prove one's salt and to set apart the heroes from the men – the Company Commander would give Karnail

---

8 The elected village management committee

9 A loose fitting long shirt and pajamas

10 Turbans

not only a fair chance – but the most daring and befitting opportunity to prove himself. This, his grandfather said, would be the best redemption for all the pain and anguish seen by Karnail in his early years. And the Company Commander, in the manner of a gentleman, looked into his Grandfather's eyes and nodded in affirmation.

With the Battalion being now deployed on the demanding North Eastern frontier and also the international border, it was tough on the men. The terrain was rugged and torturous. The steep mountains were un-relenting on man or beast; and the enemy snipers - unforgiving. It was now winters – a long and exacting innings for the men – with the country snow bound and temperatures dipping as low as minus 45^0 C. All the roads were closed and cut off from the rest of the world for the next three months. It was now only boundless snow, the unfeeling rocky out crops and the packs of hungry wild dogs roaming the wilderness for a kill. Nature here was at its severest. Karnail undaunted by the enemy, the terrain or the climate was upbeat and buoyant as he always was; volunteering for all the tough tasks in his outfit. He presently was deployed, in the forward most (ten men) section post – which jutted into the enemy's land like a finger in a pie (and thus rightly called the 'Finger'). It was a most vulnerable and daunting task to be holding this forward position – under the constant watch and surveillance of the enemy on all sides. In a period of a month, the enemy had already mounted two unsuccessful raids on the 'Finger' - each time to be surprised by alert men and facing accurate return fire. Karnail of course was the source of perseverance of his section.

Then one night a snow blizzard raged, the one that howls and cries and blows the sharp grains of snow at forceful speeds. This weather was not right for the men on the 'Finger'. It was a time ripe for the enemy to come up with any surprises that had been stored up his sleeve, for just this kind of opportunity. The post was on a round the clock alert and a constant vigil. And then the sound of enemy's automatic long range fire broke through the crying blizzard – but this time instead of at the 'Finger', it was their adjoining company post – the 'Ring Contour', on which the enemy had mounted his raid. Karnail and his section listened to the sounds with close attention, differentiating the enemy fire from their own weapons. Both sides were firing hard - and the otherwise silent reserve frequencies (radio frequencies used only when 'in contact' with enemy) were now teeming with heavy transmission from the 'Ring Contour'. Though it was not them but their neighbouring company post which was under attack, Karnail knew well the heat of the hour – having seen it through two times over. Moreover he knew each and every man on the Ring Contour that day. He had his old cronies there; those with whom he had trained and trudged miles together. The firing now had been going on for about forty minutes, when 'Finger' received an encrypted and urgent radio transmission from the Company Commander himself – Ring Contour was dangerously low on machine gun ammunition – and what little they had was fast running out. They urgently needed a replenishment to beat back the enemy attack. And no one else, but the men at 'Finger' being the closest were best poised to provide this aid. They had to pack as much of the machine gun ammunition as was available with them and send an immediate link (of two men) to the pre-decided rendezvous (RV) (coordinated in advance for such eventualities) – where a similar link would meet them from the 'Ring Contour'. And then at the end of the message – the Company Commander added - that one of the men in the link would have to be Sepoy Karnail Singh. Karnail smiled – he was already finished with lacing his boots and putting on his snow jacket, even before the Company Commander's instructions were fully received.

When the two men started from the 'Finger' – the blizzard was still raging and the snow hit the face like loose gravel from a freshly laid road. Karnail and his buddy started out well equipped and with their loads tightly packed on their shoulders. It was a treacherous descent into a very deep *nallah*[11] and then an equally steep climb over a vertical rock face – which lay between them and their RV. Though they had rehearsed navigating to the RV many a times before; but today the ominous sky and the exceptionally thick blanket of snow made the landscape appear all new and uncharted. It was in the initial descent itself that Karnail's friend lost his foot hold and slipped over the rocks. Having twisted his ankle there was no way he could go any further. As per the existing procedure, Karnail alone couldn't proceed any further too; in fact the threat of hypoxia (in the prevailing sub-zero temperatures) and the hungry wild dogs - had let it be made a rule that a minimum of at least two men went out anywhere together. So, Karnail would now have to message back to his post, and wait till two other men arrived to relieve them. This meant a long and undesirable delay; especially so when the lives of men at 'Ring Contour' were so precariously poised. But then message back to his post - he did, so that his injured colleague could be escorted back to safety. As for him (he thought) - breaking a rule would never be so much fun again, and if not now than when. With that he took the ammunition load off his friend's shoulders and

11 A crevice formed in the mountains as a result of fast flowing water

without wasting a moment, started out for the RV all alone by himself.

The load being double of what a soldier would ideally carry and the heavy snow having fully obliterated the important landmarks along the way, the going seemed tougher and Karnail was almost fainting with exhaustion. His sweat and the breath he exhaled had crystallized on his moustache and beard, his shoulders had long gone numb and he couldn't feel his feet anymore. Only one thing remained foremost in his consciousness – to keep climbing till he reached the RV. The sound of firing was now coming through to him loud and clear; disappointingly however, it was more of the enemy's weapons that he heard rather than his own. He was growing anxious and increased his pace, till he was now almost running. And finally, breaking over the top of the cliff – he reached 'Black Rock' – the designated RV. The link from 'Ring Contour' was already there; and they were surprised to see Karnail hauling such a heavy load all by himself and the extreme exhausted condition he was in. However, the ammunition was quickly handed–over along with a few encouraging words from Karnail for his friends. And resting a while, Karnail got moving back to this post.

The firing was still on at 'Ring Contour' and Karnail prayed silently under his breath (offering a prayer to Guru Gobind Singh - the tenth Guru of the Sikhs, to give courage and strength to his comrades and bless them with his invincible grace). He remembered his prayers well from childhood, when he would regularly visit the village *Gurudwara*[12] on Sundays. In the next thirty minutes as he descended the escarpment he had finished saying his prayers too. And

---

12 The place of worship of the Sikhs

now as he listened, he couldn't hear the firing any more. The sky was dark too; no more mortar bombs exploded in the sky. This silence was rueful - meaning either ways – that is, either the 'Ring Contour' had fallen (along with each of his colleague) or the enemy had been crushed – made to pay with his blood and punished for the misadventure. It was only a matter of time that they would all know of the outcome. And then suddenly, Karnail's hand-held radio set crackled with transmission from the 'Ring Contour' – only one word was being repeated emphatically – 'FATEH', 'FATEH', 'FATEH'... Karnail's heart leapt with joy. This was the coded success signal of their battalion – known well to each man. The enemy had thus been laid to rest. Made to learn a bitter lesson he easily wouldn't forget. And also Karnail caught a bit of transmission about the machine gun ammunition having reached just in the nick of time. Uplifted in spirit, Karnail gathered his strength and eagerly looked forward to being back at his post.

A few stars were now up in the sky and a wind was blowing in from the west. The snow reflected brightly with the little light from the night sky and this made his head swim. The mercury had dropped a bit more too. It was cold - freezing cold - and the clothes beneath Karnail's snow jacket were already drenched with sweat. He could feel their wetness clinging to his body. If he didn't move faster he had a chance of getting into serious trouble. The unrelenting wind, like the last dying breath of the blizzard was now going over the country. For no apparent reason, it suddenly reminded Karnail of his early morning walks in the mustard fields in his village; the wind was cold there too, but then it had a healthy freshness. And just like the boundless snow all around him; in his village too was a vast expanse of yellow mustard – as far as the eye could see. And then he wondered of his Grandfather; and how his life might be unfolding in the village. Karnail knew what his Grandfather was busy up to these days – it was the search for a bride for Karnail, which had given a new lease of life and a youthful purpose to his aging Grandfather. But then Karnail jerked his mind back to where he was and concentrated once more on not losing his foothold. He thought he heard a low bark from the rocks above. He paused and listened, but now it was quiet again – just the bottomless silence of a cold night under a dark sky.

The men at 'Finger' waited a miserably long time, but Karnail didn't turn up. Neither was there any transmission from the radio set that he had carried. The mood at 'Finger' was now growing grim. All the waiting having been done, a message was now relayed to the Battalion Head Quarters. Three search parties were immediately launched to comb the area. And finally after eighteen hours of looking around and then trailing the blood marks on the snow – they found a badly mangled and mutilated human body - lying three fourths eaten away behind a big boulder. The body though was unrecognizable; the name on the front of the snow jacket read – Sepoy Karnail Singh. To say that it broke the heart of the battalion would not be an exaggeration. Karnail Singh was a name every man knew, in whichever post he may be. Five wild dogs lay dead next to Karnail; two whose jaws had been torn apart and three whose necks had been twisted and broken. From the footprints it was clear that there had been a total of about eight to nine wild dogs in the pack that had closed around Karnail that night and had brutally hunted him down.

Karnail's neck had been torn away and nothing remained of his face. The limbs too were exposed to the bones, and a gaping hole stood, where the torso should have been. The picture of an exhausted Karnail – already spent with his arduous fatigue – now being attacked by a pack of wild dogs; was revoltingly sickening and heart rending to imagine. Karnail - the life of his team was now dead. It didn't seem right. In fact it was horribly ugly as to how the things had turned out to be. For a lion to be hunted by the dogs – was surely an abominable blunder of fate. The Company Commander was sick in the stomach; and the men at 'Finger' - indignant, foul and remorseful – all at the same time. The news spread like fire through the whole battalion and an indescribable remorse suffocated each man who heard of the incident. It seemed like an excessively raw deal, served out to the most daring of the players.

Also by now, as part of the After Action Review, a record of the enemy's radio transmissions and coded messages (intercepted – both during the course of, and post-skirmish) were also being deciphered and analysed by the Radio Interpretation Cell. 'Unbelievable' it was, in the enemy's own words – that just when the machine guns at Ring Contour had fallen silent and the 'bayonet charge' was about to commence – that a timely reinforcement (out of the blues and in such unfavorable weather) had materialized for the defender. The blazing machine guns spewing lead had once more held off the enemy. And this, the enemy ascribed, as the single most cause of their failed raid on Ring Contour.

And then the Commanding Officer; who himself was a man of great reason and understanding – heard from the Company Commander – first hand – of how the link (against the Standing Instructions on the subject) – had been carried out all alone by Karnail. It didn't take long for all to learn (including the enemy too) – that it was this one man's indomitable grit that had saved the day for Ring

Contour (and had turned a defeat into victory), that fateful night.

Karnail rightfully was hailed a hero and a martyr's homage paid next morning – to the memory of the man who had made his wager and set a new benchmark of personal valour in the battalion.

As per the procedure being followed due to the tough terrain and the high altitude deployment, Karnail was given a hero's funeral at his post itself and his frugal belongings; that is his prayer book, a few photographs with his Grandfather, a photograph of his mother, a sticker of Guru Gobind Singh, a pair of clothes and his mess tin were sent to his village, along with his ashes and mortal remains, with two men from his Company. They also carried a brief summary of his gallant action and a 'Certificate of Valour' issued by the Commanding Officer. This was handed over to his Grandfather in front of the whole village.

A man passing away in a village is not a big affair; but a hero's ashes arriving with full military honours, happens only very rarely. While his Grandfather and his friends did try to stand tall, but the ground had sunk a little that day and the flow of tears from their eyes couldn't be stopped.

Our friend is now folklore. And much in the way of gunpowder, the mere mention of his name instantly ignites a thousand men. And even today, the school teachers in Jangpura while remembering Karnail and recollecting his gallant action, do not forget to tell the young children that - 'A brave man never goes un-noticed in his life'.

And if ever you chance to visit the lines of the Bravo Company of the Eighth Battalion of the Sikhs, you will find Karnail's name etched high above, in golden ink, on the 'Martyr's Board' in the 'Heroes Gallery'.

Joy of the Journey Lies in Travelling

(They said he had struggled a lot in his life and then had finally succeeded in making a very big fortune. For several years everything ran smoothly like his Lamborghini; until one day he lost it all with one wrong business deal. The man was now a recluse, but strangely enough, everyone called him the 'sage'. I don't know if he was in his senses or if he was drunk, when he told me that)

'Most of the time, wherever we look we find people preparing themselves for the future, struggling all the time, saving all the money and planning and setting future goals for themselves. All this with so much intensity and seriousness, that most of the life goes past in preparing oneself to live rather than having lived well. We somehow always seem to forget that the joy of the journey lies in travelling and not in having arrived.

It is like the case of the Rainbow. Instead of enjoying the miracle and beauty of the rainbow and feasting our eyes and heart on it, we most often wonder about the jackpot which is proclaimed to be buried at the end of it.

But what we miss out is that each rainbow is ephemeral in appeal and that the real jackpot lies not at the end, but is spread all over it in the form of seven glorious colours. Just to behold a rainbow is to have found the jackpot; we however always miss this fact.

Like a family where a son finally gets a job after years of struggle, but his father, though he has a bottle of champagne, doesn't pop the cork, but plans to do so at his daughter's wedding. How foolish man is, he thinks of the future with so much certainty when he cannot even predict the outcome of the next few moments. It is this sad reason why so many bottles of champagne remain unopened and so many a celebration never kick-off, because they are postponed for some greater occasions in the indefinite realm of future.

How many a wife never savours the thrill and joy which lies in being gifted a rose, a chocolate, a bottle of perfume, a hair clip or a beauty soap from their husband; who though he loves her intensely but is saving all the money to buy her a big diamond ring. That is after he has saved enough to buy a car, build a house and marry the daughter. Those smiles which his wife could have smiled or those tears of joy which she could have shed are far too expensive to be bet on some large diamond ring or heavy gold chain, planned to be bought in the unforeseeable future.

Why don't we realize that a small flower in our hand today is a much greater treasure than the largest diamond or the longest car which we may or may not have in the future? Why has God not given man the power and wisdom to enjoy and make the most of what he has? Instead of just planning and planning and planning for the future.

And when the future comes? Will this man be still around?

And most often, even when the future arrives, man is unable to recognize it and celebrate. To him it still seems the present and he further prepares.

I wish we all could understand that the only truth is this moment as we breathe and nothing else. Real life is lived in seconds and minutes and not in years or decades. If we could somehow understand this, each meeting with our lovers would be a Valentine's Day and each moment with our partners would be an anniversary. Just close your eyes and imagine what an entirely different place this world would be and how much more love and happiness would there be all around.'

Blinking

In the country that I visited last year on vacation I witnessed a strange phenomenon. As I sat sipping my espresso on the main esplanade - I saw a cat cross the road from the opposite end and collide head-on with a lamp post next to my table. Dazed, it got up and crossed the road back again. The same afternoon I saw another cat on the top of a tall building. It walked slowly to the edge of the roof and there pausing with uncertainty, it looked around. Then taking a small step, it fell six stories below and broke its neck on the pavement. The next case was of two mangy dogs walking down an empty street – with a cat watching them from the other end. I waited to see the dogs being outrun by the cat and made a fool of. But the cat unblinking, just kept staring at the face of death and moved not an inch; until the dogs were upon her and (most unceremoniously) almost unhinged her body and soul – but for my last minute intervention. Spared its life, the cat shot like a bullet – only to run straight into a big garbage bin and pass out. Holy Christ! Was it blind? And then comes along an old lady with her two pet cats – walking them on a leash. Cats – and on a leash? Well I myself never heard of it before. Not even from the mad servant boy; who narrated me the weirdest of stories when I was a kid. And then the old lady, on my polite insistence, let me know that her cats were blind; just like all other cats everywhere - in the town, the county, the state and the country. And then it all fell into place, only to leave me wondering of the strangeness of my discovery. The cats everywhere were blind – How could this possibly come to be? The cab driver answered my dilemma by telling me how this was the result of an officially undertaken exercise in his country. "What does one gain by it?" I asked. To which he said "I'll let you know after dinner". Later that day as we drove out to witness the city's night life, I reminded the driver of his pending reply. "Well, so that at night we don't lose our way" he said. And then pointing ahead – he drew my attention to the little red lights that blinked on either sides of the road, all the way up into the darkness. All the roads in the country were thus lined he said; to ensure that one never lost his way at night. These blinking lights he added "Of course were the Cat's eyes". They were a marvel to the eye – how they blinked unto yonder and made the road look like a twinkling river in the deep darkness. But then since all the cats had long gone blind, no new roads got made in the country for a very long time. Only now that a solution had been found – several new highways were under construction, my cabbie informed. "And pray, what is the solution you've found?" I asked. "We're starting with the dogs!" he gravely replied.

Simple Joys...

1. Turning out a perfect brown toast from your electric toaster.

2. To find an old transistor working, which you thought was junk by now.

3. Finding the right key and opening a lock - in the very first attempt out of a huge bunch of keys.

4. In winters, being able to mix the right water for your bath.

5. Brewing out a perfect tea - when tired.

6. Your car stereo suddenly auto-tuning to a favourite old melody.

7. Unexpectedly finding the perfect parking space in a very tight and crowded market.

8. Quickly finding the perfect fragrance (which you have been long looking for), in a large perfume store.

9. Your car making it to the petrol station, when the petrol is out and you least expect it to.

10. Finding a beautiful travelling companion on the adjacent seat in the plane.

11. Finding an un-occupied toilet in a crowded shopping mall, when you can't hold your bladder anymore.

12. Your suitcase turning out first on the luggage conveyor belt at the arrival terminal.

13. Getting your desired choice of shoe and the right size, at a 70% clearance sale.

14. Your wife forgetting to nag you on a Sunday.

15. When you are the first one to bathe with a new soap placed in the bathroom.

16. When your wait-listed railway ticket, unexpectedly gets confirmed an hour before departure.

17. As you hurry to dress up for a party - your tie turns out at the perfect length, in the very first attempt.

18. On reaching office you learn that your boss has suddenly had to proceed on a week's leave without leaving any instructions for you.

19. Even though you are late and the bank is beginning to shut down - they allow you to draw cash, as the last customer of the day.

20. While rushing for a movie you are delayed in traffic; only to find on arrival that the movie is yet to start owing to a technical snag.

21. The doctor goes through all your investigations and finally tells you - that nothing's seriously wrong. It was only an anxiety attack, and you have got to slow down.

22. Watching a beautiful sunset.

23. Getting to the swimming pool on a bright and sunny afternoon, to find you are the first one to arrive.

24. Experiencing the season's first snow fall.

25. On reaching you find the gym crowded but your favourite cross-trainer un-occupied.

26. Feeding ducks in the park.

27. Getting wet in the first monsoon shower.

28. Writing your name on your car's frosted window.

29. Getting to use the stapler when there is only the last pin left.

30. Finding the ketchup bottle empty, yet with just enough ketchup at the bottom to go with your plate of french fries.

The Color Was Black

It was a busy corporate life where one had to keep running fast, just to remain in one's place. There was no time for luxuries like books, movies, TV, friends, bath-tubs etc. Having had to change three jobs in four years and being in-waiting for eight months in between (with the regular expenses of a new wife, old parents, house rent, electricity bills, petrol, cigarettes etc), had introduced an element of uncertainty in Abhishek's life. All protective layers having gradually peeled away – his nerves were now raw, exposed to the elements and instantly touched by any (howsoever remote) looming disapproval of the bosses. Lest it leads to another laying-off and a fresh old struggle to sell one's employability in an already saturated market.

It was located on the ninth floor. A pre-fabricated office - made up of cubicles of soft board, half-way high from the floor (allowing for private working space only waist downwards!), where employees sat back to back, breathing each other's lifeless breath and fixated to their computer monitors. The elevator delivered them all from the earth's womb every morning; taking them to their suspended working world (nine floors above) and in the evening deposited them back. Where they started the engines of their waiting time-machines and returned once more into the other half of their lives.

It was already dark. The work day had gone tough and Abhishek felt like a squeezed lemon. The continued stress of the day's hectic activities had sapped away his energies and quite almost numbed his brain. It had been a week of long hours spent in the office, and today it was not just the day's load straining him but the accumulated pressure of the whole week gone by.

It was sickening to witness all successive days falling into the same pre-ordained pattern, and each ending with the same exhaustion. But today it would be different. Was it not all in the mind, as claimed by the new age gurus? Enough of being a captive to one's constraints, enough of the endemic environment and enough of being pulled down by regular routine stuff. Today it would not be getting down to drinks as usual. This was no way for the days to pass by.

Rather than slumping into the rear seat of the black company SUV, Abhishek waived the driver aside and decided to take the wheel himself. The distance from his office to the rented Paying Guest accommodation was a mere twenty kilometers and he was well versed with both - the peculiarities of the SUV and the potholes along the road. The mechanics of driving a vehicle and the attentiveness required, quite often served to divert his mind from the dullness and exhaustion of the day.

Just as the key fired the ignition, his mobile began to vibrate. Being tired of the endless calls and the meaningless conversations, Abhishek cursed and let the damn thing just be. The bastard at the other end didn't give up, whoever he may have been. The mobile vibrated with five back to back calls, without being answered - today was different. One thing Abhishek liked about driving was that no matter how hassled and hurried you may be, there were no shortcuts. You had to follow the same basic rules to get your car moving. It helped in getting you back to the actual speed of life and bringing your mind to rest by focusing on the very basics i.e. shifting gears, giving an indicator, cutting a fine turn, avoiding a pothole, slowing for a speed breaker and so on.

Putting the vehicle into gear and slowly releasing the clutch, he got the car moving and relaxed in his seat - allowing his mind to shift gears as well. The days were beginning to get longer, summer was creeping in. While his shift got over at the same time as always - it was not as dark as before. The sky was clear and aglow with hues of orange and the soft glow of a setting sun. A gentle breeze played with the leaves of the neem trees and the bougainvillea bushes along the road. A bunch of college students walked by on the pavement, the magic of the evening putting a spring into their steps. A road side vendor was pouring tea into the glass tumblers on his tray, while his customers waited on miniature cane stools next to his make shift stall. This was the place where Abhishek had to leave the main road and turn right - into the side street to his rented accommodation. He expertly maneuvered the turn.

The street at this time was deserted as usual. A cab crossed him from the opposite direction, honking as it went by (for no apparent reason). A black poly bag lying in the middle of the road fluttered with the breeze. As the distance reduced, the bag fluttered a little more. And just as the SUV closed in, the black poly bag shook and lifted up from the ground, as if coming alive. Was it just a poly bag or perhaps a bit more? He braked, simultaneously catching glimpse of a black puppy scurrying on its feet - but not quite getting out of the way. SUVs' are heavy machines; they don't brake to a halt for fluttering poly bags or similar size of things. Abhishek hoped like hell that the puppy had escaped unhurt. But the uneven roll of the SUV and the dull thud of the wheel passing over and crushing something were intensely sickening. Bringing the vehicle to a halt, he got down.

Looking back, he the saw the puppy's crushed head. It's frail body still quivering. And a thick black liquid - lazily draining away from its head. There was not even a whimper or a faint cry. The puppy's head was crushed and leveled on the black bitumen - taking him from slumber to a sudden awakening, and back into darkness. The road was deserted, not a person around. No witnesses. No cause for guilt. No obligation for remorse, and no reason to look back. The driver on the passenger seat remaining indifferent and saying nothing, then only 'Sahib, let's go'.

Abhishek stood fixed in the middle of the road, still looking back; growing conscious of the strange hollow and sinking feeling within his chest. Everything was so bloody disgusting. And now this nausea was beginning to get to him. He felt he would throw up any instant. Meanwhile, dusk had given way to darkness. And despite the cool breeze, his head spun and everything seemed to go black.

Thoughts raced in Abhishek's head. Was it something so big that had happened today? Was it not just a small dog? Was it entirely his fault? Had he done it knowingly? Why had the dog to be there in the middle of the road? Then he found him telling himself, that he had not killed it purposefully. It was just an accident. So what if it had happened - Wasn't he sorry now? Wasn't this more than enough? Should he pay with his own life or what? With one dog less, does it change anything? Wasn't this between two dogs today - one in the SUV and the other on the road? Both exhausted and in a haze, both taken by surprise; and none of them wanting any of this. But one of them just had to go this day. Isn't this how it happens sometimes?

From there on, the driver took the car. That evening, Abhishek went back to his drinks as usual; went back once more - to slouching in his sofa and looking out at the city lights from his seventh floor window. It had been a long day. Although he was against making any decisions over drinks, but then, two things were decided from today - Firstly, he would not be making any more resolutions about changing his pattern of life. And secondly, he would not be taking to the wheel on his return from office any more.

Travelling Companions

(An ode to my worthy co-passengers)

Aunty

We the passengers of the *Shatabdi* Express waited eagerly for Benares. Not because we were particularly religious; but because it was getting to be 9 pm and we were all looking forward to our dinner. It was at Benares Railway Station that our dinner trays were to be collected by the railway catering staff. The approaching city lights could now be seen through the thick winter fog. And then the train pierced through the town; the town which seemed to have stretched and stopped just short of the railway tracks. The halt at Benares was a brief one and as the train pulled away, the last remaining berth in our compartment was taken up by a new passenger - Aunty. Aunty in her late forties was short, plump, wrapped up in a *sari*[13], a thick cardigan, a shawl and to top it up - a pink fur cap (with the word 'baby'

[13] A South Asian female garment consisting of a length of cotton or silk elaborately draped around the body

embroidered on its front); which was pulled over her ears and covered her entire forehead and eye brows too. From the looks of Aunty – she appeared to be profusely married, exceedingly weather beaten and a mother of at least four children. She carried more luggage than the balance of us three passengers in the compartment. Aunty with her chunky arms, lifted, pushed and shoved away all her heavy bags (into place) within less than two minutes. The only piece of her baggage which she placed squarely in front of her (as she reclined and caught her breath) was a four-container steel Tiffin carrier and a white poly bag.

Even though the air conditioning inside the coach was efficient enough, Aunty didn't even as much pull away her cap from her forehead or remove any of her woolen layers (but then I have never bothered myself with the affairs of others.) As we were handed over our dinner trays and began our meal; Aunty too opened her Tiffin-carrier and started in earnest. Since mine was an upper berth I could well easily see into Auntie's Tiffin (who sat down below and diagonally across to me). Two containers were full-up to the brim with *yellow dal*[14], one container was of spiced curd and the fourth was topped up with fried mixed vegetables. Then from the accompanying poly bag, Aunty gently pulled out and placed in front of her a thick bundle of *rotis*[15] (at least about thirty to thirty five of them). From the amount of rations it seemed as if Aunty had embarked on a long journey (of perhaps 36 to 48 hours); and was accordingly stocked. Anyway we all proceeded with our dinners in

---

[14] A popular South Asian dish made with yellow split peas (lentils) cooked with garlic and onion

[15] Roti is an Indian Subcontinent unleavened flat bread, made from stoneground whole meal flour (wheat flour)

silence and in apt concentration (which comes naturally when one is famished). As we (the other three passengers) finished and disposed of with our dinners, Aunty was still working at it (how slowly some people eat really surprises me at times; but then it is none of my concern). Next we settled down and pulled up our blankets (except Aunty of course).

For a while I busied myself with my smart phone (recently having been forced by the kids to buy one) and cautiously explored its eccentricities. Then feeling drowsy I surrendered myself to slumber. It would have been about forty minutes (of a nap) when a sudden jolt from the braking of the train woke me up (it was a temporary halt I realized). As I peered down from my seat I saw Aunty still continuing her dinner in the glow of the reading light. Auntie's Tiffin boxes were more than half empty and I silently appreciated her appetite. She would now be winding up any instant (I guessed); even her thick bundle of *rotis* was running out. The rancid smell of her mango pickle and raw onion salad was quite strong and had permeated the whole cabin. The train set rolling once more and I fell back to sleep. I even dreamed a small and pleasant dream; where I - a millionaire - was on a magnificent holiday on a yacht with about half a dozen Kingfisher Calendar girls. Just as the climax to my holiday seemed to be coming up - the poor air conditioning in the cabin caused me to wake up. It was awfully warm and the other passengers sat up too. The attendant needed to be immediately called and asked to adjust the thermostat. It was then, that as I was about to dismount from my berth - I saw Aunty still chomping away her *rotis*. She had now been eating steadily for about an hour and a half and had kept her momentum. But then she was not one to be embarrassed and bit-off half a green chili, as

I was putting on my slippers. Soon (that is in about half an hour) the attendant came up and adjusted the thermostat; and the cabin once again grew cool. As I climbed back to my seat I saw that sweat was running down Auntie's temples and that she kept wiping her brow with the loose end of her sari. She almost panted with each morsel now and her face was quite red. It was clear that the strain of her continued eating was taking a toll on her (and had become a kind of an aerobic exercise for her). Nevertheless, she (not one to give up) finished off all the *rotis* in her bundle and then with her thick fingers licked away all the remaining sauces and oils in her empty Tiffin containers. It was a stupendous feat that Aunty had performed that night - eating fastidiously for approximately Two Full Hours!

Packing away her Tiffin in the rack above, Aunty wiped her hands and mouth (with her sari) and then perspiring heavily; lay down exhausted on her berth. And in no time she was loudly snoring and fast asleep!

Bunty

I am reminded of yet another of my travelling companion in the course of my travails in the train. It was afternoon and the heat was stupefying. I rushed through the crowded platform pulling my stroller (like a dead dog) behind me. The train had already arrived; with the scheduled halt at the station being only ten minutes. And if I missed this one, the next train to Delhi would be after twenty four hours.

These were the days when First Class coupes were still in vogue in the Indian Railways. Mine was the last two-berth cabin adjacent to the exit door of the coach. And as I boarded the train and gripped the handlebar to slide open the door to Cabin 'F' - I hoped for a young and attractive female travelling companion (why did it have to happen only with others? I wondered). But then luck didn't favor me again. As I entered the cabin, I saw a large man sprawled on the lower berth.

To classify the man simply as 'large' would be an understatement. He was astoundingly fat and in being so - was quite 'large'. His shirt buttons were all open and so his shirt (on both sides) had simply slipped off his barrel bodied frame. His chest was smooth and rather too wholesome for a male member of the genus. Both his hands lay aligned symmetrically on either sides of his body. He was clean shaven and without a moustache. The hair on his head was just about a fistful. From the looks of it he appeared to be in his late thirties. There was no item of baggage belonging to him which I could see anywhere in the cabin, not even as much as a bottle of water. His eyes were tightly shut and mouth fully open with saliva making its way out from the left side. Lying on his back without a pillow - his head fell backwards and the chin pointed to the roof of the cabin.

From the look of it my travelling companion seemed sound asleep. Since I myself am a peace loving and a live-and-let-live kind of a fellow - I had not the heart to wake up my fellow passenger and ask him to accommodate me on the lower berth too. With time being around twelve in the noon; I clambered up to my seat and having nothing better to do, I read the newspaper thrice. And then when I peeped below - my friend was still as sound asleep as before. Getting bored, I took out my packed lunch and was soon over with it. The senses now began to dull and the print on the newspaper appeared to be gently floating away like a slow moving river. It was time for my siesta I realized and being a strict follower of routine – I gave in to the urge.

Waking up to the calls of a *Chai wallah*[16] at the open window I noted that the train stood at a small platform and with sundown, the climate now was much cooler. I took out some change from my wallet and got down to purchase a cup of tea for me. To my deep surprise, my friend was still fast asleep. He hadn't moved even a millimeter from his initial position and had exactly the same expressionless face as before. I glanced at my watch and saw the needles ticking past 5:30 pm. I wondered if my companion was so tired as to not even have moved a finger or heard the *Chai wallah* hollering over his head.

It was with great difficulty that I (all alone and without having anyone to talk to) bided away my time till around 9 pm. The sight of my unmoving companion, however, now seemed un-nerving and was causing me a strange bewilderment. When the pantry boy walked-in to hand me over my dinner - I asked him if he had seen my fellow passenger awake during any of his earlier visits. He replied in the negative and said that my friend had been sleeping in exactly the same fashion since 6 am in the morning; when he had come around to hand him over his bed tea (and had simply left the tea under the seat). The same was true for lunch as well. And the stuff all lay below my co-passenger's seat (where it could still be seen). Having said this, the pantry boy vanished.

My antennas were now up and I suddenly smelled a rat. Lying unmoving for more than fifteen hours! Had my friend been drugged and burgled? Or had he had a heart attack or been poisoned? Or worse still, was he dead? This and a chain of other such ominous thoughts raced through my head. I came down slowly from my berth and

---

[16] A tea vendor

first ensured that the cabin door was bolted from inside. Then I crept close to my travelling companion and peered intently into his face. It could not have been any more alive than a piece of stone. I looked for the flaring of his nostrils or the sound of air escaping his lips - but there was none. I looked closely at his chest - but it did not rise or fall even a vague bit.

If he was alive - it just didn't even remotely appear so. But what if he was dead? Was the question which scared the blooming daylights out of me! I looked around the cabin and for the first time realized - how it seemed just the perfect scene of crime. Only two passengers to begin with and one of them dead - however made to appear as if sleeping; and the other passenger appearing to be vehemently unaware and completely innocent. I had little chances either way I realized. The only escape perhaps lay in quietly getting off (unnoticed) at the next halt i.e. at the Old Delhi railway station in the morning; without the homicide having been discovered.

I saw the dinner tray on my seat but had no inclination to eat. Along with my appetite I had also lost my sleep. I shut the window and switched off the cabin light. And the whole night I sat up chanting my prayers; lest the raging spirit of my late friend - lay hold on me. Naturally to be penning it down today, implies - that I was safely delivered through that long night.

As Old Delhi approached, the morning sun was casting slanting beams of light on my dead friend's face (which was exactly as before). I quietly prepared my departure and gathered my luggage near the cabin door. The halt at Old Delhi was only five minutes and I desperately wanted to be the first passenger to dismount and melt away into the crowd at the platform. And get away before anyone discovered me to be the ill-fated occupant of Cabin 'F' and the sole travelling companion of my late friend (God Bless! his soul).

I tied my shoe laces, straightened my collar and pulled down my cap; the lesser visible my face - the better for me I thought. As the sun grew bold the scene of the crime was getting brighter. Thankfully - the slums and shanties of Old Delhi began to appear astride the railway tracks and I could now see early risers defecating in the open. Old Delhi was closing in from all sides and given the circumstances, even an innocent man felt morbid fear today. Other people in the coach had begun to shift their luggage in the passage too. And with this the train arrived on the platform.

Surprisingly, it seemed as if the whole world was gathered out there this morning to witness some strange drama. But I couldn't be bothered by any of this and focused only on melting away into the crowd. As soon as the train halted, I pulled on my cabin door to slide it open, but it seemed some goddamn idiot in the corridor had piled his heavy baggage against it - and the door was jammed! And now with no place to hide or get away from; rivers of sweat broke forth from every pore of my body. I even saw a policeman on the platform. And just when it couldn't have got any worse, an old man's head appeared at my cabin window - frantically trying to peer inside and shouting "Bunty! Bunty!" And then again "Bunty! Bunty!"

And then before I could say Jack Robinson! or even blink my bleary eyes – 'Bunty' - my long dead and deceased travelling companion - jumped up like a startled hare and jerking open the cabin door (and in that pushing me aside) - had scrambled over the heads of the passengers and was gone away with the old man in an instant. It happened faster than a bullet travels from a barrel of a gun or a streak of lightning flashes in the sky; that 'Bunty' my late travelling companion - had suddenly come back to life and had vanished in a blink.

Naturally I couldn't be caught for a crime that just escaped happening. And so that morning, I walked away scot free and live till today an innocent and an honest man!

The Girl

We were already acclimatized and travelling since half a day when our train halted at Bhopal. There as we sat looking out at the crowd on the platform - perspiring and pushing; the world inside our coach seemed far removed and thankfully serene. It was then that a whole family comprising of an aging father, a middle age mother, a boy in his early teens and a girl in her mid-twenties (siblings as evident) got into our compartment. It suddenly became awfully tight in there - as there was no room for so many passengers. Perhaps this family had come into the wrong coupe? We had only one vacant side lower seat remaining in our coach and here were four passengers who had boarded! Seeing the worried look on my face the father politely remarked "We have just come to see off our daughter and put her on the train". Of course I too smiled graciously (and did not let the sigh of relief be noticed by them) and added "Naturally I understand. That's how it is in a family" (at the same time wondering - how the whole family had nothing better to do?).

The train stuck to the schedule and blew the whistle indicating departure. The family - kissing and hugging the girl - got off one by one. And with this the train moved on, leaving us to study the new passenger and to proceed with the usual mental exercise of drawing of conclusions and forming of opinions. The young girl (age - as already mentioned earlier) first took off her sandals (by pushing them off the heels by her alternate feet), then settled on her seat and crossed her legs. She next straightened her dress (to cover both her legs) and placed her hand bag in her lap. Taking out her cellphone she checked her messages (replying to a few of them by delicately tapping her fingers on the touch screen) with the shadow of a faint smile (once or twice) and then put her phone back into her bag. She then pulled her sleeves to bring them once more up to her wrists. Next she drew back the loose strands of her hair once more into her ponytail and redid her elastic hair band. Everything about her looked far too orderly and meticulous.

In a little while the ticket examiner arrived and checked her ticket; which she returned back into a small brown pouch in her handbag. She then reclined and taking out a small and white handkerchief (with pink little flowers on it) proceeded to gently dab the corners of her mouth and remove any dust (if ever there was any?) off her face and forehead. Opening her handbag once more, she pulled out a thin green sachet. The wet tissue which she tenderly removed from the packing had a scent of fresh jasmine in it; and with this she delicately commenced to cleanse her face and neck. It was with the sensitivity and reflection of a Tai Chi expert that she used her wet tissue. Having cleansed her already clean face, she looked around for a dustbin. But not finding one, she folded the used tissue neatly and put it back in its packet and into her handbag (I guess it's only because of the discretion of a few passengers like her that the Indian Railways is still a tolerable enough mode of travel).

The girl now looked even brighter, quite like a rain-washed daisy. Not to be satisfied with just that; our travelling companion next took out a bottle of hand cleanser from her travel bag and squeezed a few drops of it into the hollow of her hand. Rubbing her hands well, the girl now seemed sanitized enough to perform a surgery on any of us; and the coupe too now smelled like an Operation Theatre (albeit with a scent of jasmine). We (the other passengers) kind of looked at each other and felt as if we belonged to the slums and lived like muck.

Anyway since no surgery could be performed on healthy passengers, our travelling companion put on her head phones and immersed herself into the world of music. Suddenly we (the others) were left looking blankly at each other and feeling acutely embarrassed to be sitting so completely idle and staring stupidly at the floor. Not knowing what to do, one of us even began to pick his nose!

While the rest of us, for dinner, gorged on deep fried '*samosas*[17]' and oily '*pakoras*[18]' from the vendors on the train; our little girl snacked only on a brown-bread sandwich and an apple (both of which she had carried in her bag). Moreover she ate it with such restraint, that (in comparison) it made us feel like pigs gone berserk on a potato farm. Then preparing to settle for the night, the girl spread out her bedding, again so neatly and methodically - that she could have put to shame, any head nurse in a hospital. While we (the others) were still exhausting ourselves over our dinner, our cleanest companion was fast sleep.

---

17 A samosa is a fried or baked pastry with savoury filling, such as spiced potatoes, onions, peas or lentils

18 Is a fried Indian snack made from either potatoes, onions, plantain, spinach or cauliflower

And since I was the first to disembark the next morning, I don't know how the balance of the journey went. But when I had last looked at her, our friend still was blissfully lost in her sterile dreams!

My Crime against a Dragonfly

(This letter one day came to the Pastor of our church. But unfortunately he never could reply to it, since the name of the originator was vague; it simply said - from a God fearing man who works in a government office)

'Dear Pastor, Please accept my under mentioned confession: I never knew who this dragonfly was or why she came to my office every day and hovered over my desk. And because most of the time I was just so busy with some useless files, that I never gave this matter a serious thought. However slowly the visits of the dragonfly began to irritate me; as I was under a false impression that I owned the space enclosed by the four walls of my office – and I saw in this dragonfly - insubordination and lack of respect for my authority.

One day while sipping tea I noticed that a slot meant for a pen in my pen stand was blocked with some white cement like dry mixture. Out of my ignorance and indifference I broke this white cement covering and peeped inside. I could see something lying beneath. I soon dug it out with a paper pin, it happened to be some small white eggs and a baby dragonfly, probably just born.

The whole mystery was revealed to me in an instant. I quickly put the eggs and the baby dragonfly back into the deep slot. However, I could not cement and cover the mouth of the slot. Now I waited eagerly for the mother dragonfly to return; hoping it would soon arrive and fix the white cement top.

In a little while, the mother dragonfly did arrive and hovered over my desk for a few seconds; and then finally landed on its home turf (that is the pen-stand). I could see some anxiety and tension in the sharp and sudden movements of the dragonfly. After her final inspection, which lasted about 30 seconds she gave one long and final peep into the pen-slot as if saying a sad good bye to her eggs and new born. Then it quickly took off, flew two circles above my head, as if sizing me up and made an exit through the office door.

The next day, the day after and the whole week, I waited anxiously for the mother dragonfly to return; but it never came back. Meanwhile a friend made me wiser by telling me that once its nest has been disturbed, a dragonfly abandons it forever. The observation seemed true, as the mother dragonfly never returned. Slowly the baby dragonfly died and small white termites ate away the eggs.

Today when I think back of that hot summer afternoon; I can see that when the dragonfly flew out of my office for the last time that day, it not only left behind its ransacked home and dead children but an utterly despicable and an unfeeling murderer sitting behind a bunch of useless files.'

A Good Country

It was a Good Country and naturally the people had to be good too. They conformed to the rules of the game with extreme passion. The social activists, the philanthropists, the charitable trusts, the land mafias, the under-world dons, the serial rapists, the psychotic killers, the legendary con-men, the reputed hawala operators, the revered drug cartels, and the corrupt politicians - all remained tirelessly engaged and dedicated to their chosen cause. Each of theirs life was full of fervor, passion and purpose. They all ran full steam, like powerful locomotive engines – each on their own track. The dictum – whatever is worth doing, is worth doing well; seemed to be the guiding beacon, for all classes of men.

It would be grossly wrong to suspect that some amongst the masses lived aimlessly. It just couldn't be. Every man or beast, breathed with a unique resoluteness and grit, remaining unflinching in his personal pursuit. It was a Country worth visiting - a popular destination for the international tourist. Movies, cars, clothes, cocaine, coffins and chocolates were perpetually flooding the markets. An unparalleled style and an unabashed attitude were the mark of each man. No man was less than his neighbor. No one knew who the middle class was. And each man was the cream of his own society.

For such a country to be shining, making swift progress and running profitably for everyone was a miracle. Here no one got into anyone's way. It was a perfect example of a community driven by the power of each man's individual commitment (i.e. the criminal's commitment to crime, the policemen's commitment to keeping their eyes closed, the leader's commitment to corruption and the mass's commitment to losing hope). Each man concocted, schemed, served or sinned with unfailing passion.

Every man was an asset, and each contributed to his class. In a country known so far, only for its mogul monuments; the drug addicts, the orphans, the destitute, the naga sadhus, the widows, the organ donors, the flesh traders and the likes of them, were the attractions of the modern age. It was an amazingly accommodating country; allowing for the freedom of any imaginable or un-imaginable religion, thought, speech, habit or practice held dear by its impassioned citizens. Or a liberal society you may say - allowing each man's outrageous dream to become a reality, and allowing everyone to get away with everything. And with the next generation seemingly smarter; the future too, looked secure and bright. Thus there was no cause for concern.

I don't know how the things would now be? But the last that I was there, it was a Good Country.

Passing By

(Haven't we all travelled so much in our lives? But then this is how a friend described a bus ride he had once taken)

'I had been travelling in this crowded bus for a very long time; overcrowded to be precise. And along with being caught up in the crowd, I was stuck in the aisle too; sometimes being pushed forward and sometimes to the rear. At other times I was falling over or being shoved at from all sides. Caught in the crowd, I sweated and could feel the sweat of others rubbing onto me as well. I could see nothing outside the bus. There was this crowd all around - some people seemed amiable, while some I despised. Then, when perhaps two thirds of the journey had been travelled, I don't know how it came to be, but as if by a miracle - suddenly finding an empty seat, I threw myself at it. Much to my relief, I was now comfortably seated and looking out of the window.

Having found a corner, I felt far removed from the dirty and perspiring crowd of the bus and somehow, none of it mattered any more. Everything now seemed to be distant and drowned in silence. The cacophony of the constant struggle had been turned mute and it felt as if I was all alone in the bus. It seemed as if the wheel of time had suddenly stopped or had slowed down a great deal. I, for a change, was beginning to get a grip on things and could see and understand a little, as to how the journey had been un-folding all this while. I was also beginning to visualize, as to how the scenery outside would have been, while I was stuck in the aisle.

It seemed rather strange and beyond my understanding, that all this while – while getting a window seat had been the sole purpose of my existence; having found one - I was not as excited as I would have liked to be. Even though I was now comfortable, without the crowd falling over me or breathing down my neck - the scenery outside seemed to have lost its charm. It didn't seem as breathtaking or even half as attractive as I had earlier believed. There was nothing new to the eye; nothing to be excited about or to be taken by surprise. It was just as the world is, nothing more and nothing less.

By now there were however a little changes in my own perspective – for instance – the bumps, the ditches and the speed breakers did not seem as severe as before. They did not shake me the same way as in the past. Now even when the road was bad, I was cursing much less or hardly at all, as compared to the earlier part of the journey.

With two thirds of the journey seemingly over, and quite a few passengers having already got off at their destinations; the crowd was now much thinner and there seemed to be no risk to my window seat. Even while the scenery outside was changing, I had grown more accustomed to observing the climate within. With the passengers constantly getting on and off, I hardly recognized them anymore. It was only sometimes that I saw a familiar face. The co-passengers in fact didn't interest me much, neither the new nor the familiar.

As I took a moment to look around the bus - I saw a few of my friends and close ones sitting there too. I suddenly thought of all the individual journeys that each of us was travelling. Were we together? Or were we all alone? Or perhaps, just co-passengers - sharing a part of each other's small journey. I all of a sudden, for no apparent reason, felt a bit afraid and un-anchored. There was a gust of cold wind from the window and some dust flew into my face.

Suddenly the driver blew the horn. I was shaken out of my musings and was back in the present moment. I tightened my grip on the cold iron handle bar and glanced outside once more. I was presumably enjoying the change in scenery. The thick and mysterious forests had given way to meadows, and one could now look far and unto the horizon.

It was my first time on that route. I really didn't know when my stop would come, perhaps just after – where the old man standing in front of me would get down? Or the lady next to him? I couldn't say with certainty. But for now there was a rush; a few passengers almost fell over. I could see in their eyes - a burning desire to get to a window seat. Strangely, I felt no hatred or bitterness towards the crowd anymore.

The journey was really intriguing. I wish I could have shared my thoughts with others, but they all appeared pre-occupied - someone having a sandwich, someone on the phone, someone on the face book, someone watching a movie, someone taking care of his baggage and someone eyeing a seat.

Though I was not yet fully exhausted, but the monotony of the travelling was beginning to get to me. I guess what I needed was not a long sleep, but only a short nap.'

The Fairer Species

In general, they take your breath away. In particular, each is unique in flavor - just like the different cocktails in a bar. Some are mildly intoxicating like gin and tonic. Some are strong like vodka. Some go down smoothly like an old cognac. Some are oversweet like a new wine. While some like arrack or raw country liquor may burn your insides. A few on the other hand are simply unpredictable, like fruit punch!

Some of them cause a little sweating in the palms and hasten the pace of one's heartbeat. Some like amphetamine evoke within you a visible nervousness, anxiety and a tendency of behaving out of your skin. Some by sheer habit wear a perfume which is impossible to resist. Some of them make you want to get young once again, or be single once more to woo them. Some make you feel an old shared connection. Some are adorable and cute. While some - simply trigger the testosterone.

Then there are those who are straight forward and fair. That is, they let it be clearly understood as to what their position or status is i.e. in the affairs of the heart and mind (i.e. whether they are engaged, married, interested, not-interested, available, not-available etc). However there are others who send confusing or mixed signals. Not realizing the disastrous consequences of such miscommunication.

Then there is a kind which is stunningly impressive in visual and sensory appeal, but lacks miserably in intelligence and verbal skills. This makes for a very pitiable impasse (imagine having broilers for pets!). Then there are others, who, while being earnestly intelligent, bubbly, and engaging in their conversation, have totally missed the bus for looks and physical proportionality. They may attempt at engaging you and holding your attention; but then vinegar is no substitute for wine (moreover, it's not practical keeping expired tinned food in your kitchen cabinet, just because you like the print on the labels).

So, it's tough. While you may easily fix a drink for another, getting it right for yourself is really tough. Just because you are adventurous, doesn't mean you can have tequila shots every day, for the rest of your life. You need something which goes with your system in the long run.

Cheers!

Wonder if it's true

As they sat together in the green and wide city park, in the *Nizam's* old town and after they had tired their eyes with watching the girls, and tired their necks from turning and tired their brains with the impossible fantasies of youth, Akram took out a pack of imported cigarettes, the long and brown menthol flavored ones – the 'Benson & Hedges' (that rather looked more like drinking straws), which are a favorite in London; and then he also took out a box of matches – straight from Yorkshire - the ones that give a bright English flame - when lighted in the parks of Hyderabad. He then offered a smoke to Nadim. Nadim rolled the cigarette over in his fingers, smelled its foreign tobacco and noted the fanciful crest just above the filter. He felt a sudden gratitude and kinship for the British workers who had rolled this cigarette, back in the factory in England. Akram next, almost in the manner of a ceremony, carefully lighted a match from the – 'Light My Fire' strip (each of the matches in the strip needed to be judiciously lit for making a subtle British impact on the chosen twenty four occasions). The cigarette having been lit and the sweet tobacco smoke inhaled by both; Akram waited for Nadim to ask the question (stories narrated without being asked generally robbed them of their mystery and charm; and so he waited, feigning a self-absorbed demeanor). And then finally, Nadim asked Akram how the latter's vacation to England had been (of course he knew it would have been magnificent – just like the cream and strawberries at Wimbledon; but then it had to be asked and heard - with the Oohs! and the Aahs!; or else he would be denying a close friend like Akram the final satisfaction of a foreign holiday), and what all he'd done in London and the fun that he had had (and even though he knew that it had to be boating on the Thames, a mug of Costa coffee at Piccadilly, a visit to 10 Downing Street, tour of the Madame Tussauds, change of guard at the Buckingham Palace etc; but then it had to be asked and heard - with the accompaniments as I have earlier said).

Having generally heard it all, Nadim now asked Akram to tell him the singular most interesting experience from his entire holiday; the one that stood out above all others (and while he knew that it had to be this or that, or that or this; but then it had to be asked). Akram took a long drag of the cigarette, feeling the smoke rising slowly to his lungs and savored the gentle and soft easiness within his head. And then with a feeling of lightness, he recollected it all and smiled. Reminiscing the memory, he narrated to Nadim the following genuinely English experience from his holiday (in case you wonder how I know; let me tell you that this very precise moment, I happened to be lying down on the bench just behind where the two friends sat. How I happened to be there, or as to what I was doing in the park all alone, is the matter of another story).

Back in Southall, Mohsin, Akram's first cousin who had been born, brought up and staying in London all since (and whom Akram was visiting) took Akram one evening to an English tailor in Savile Row; to have an English suit stitched for him - as a very special gift to his *Hyderabadi* cousin. And while going so from his house to the shop, Mohsin allowed Akram - whom he knew to be a lover of automobiles, to drive his Vauxhall Corsa (an exclusively English car). Despite it being a right hand drive car, Akram drove well and with ease. Making their way down the winding New Burlington Street, they now reached the busy piazza. The rush of people here was phenomenal, and Akram found it exceedingly difficult to park (and the Corsa is not so small a car) without bumping a British national. However, he managed it quite satisfactorily. The parking was badly crowded (for a change reminding him of Hyderabad) and Akram wondered how they were going to get their car out of it – perhaps he should let Mohsin drive the car back, he thought. The tailor recognized Mohsin and tipped his hat in a polite greeting. The elderly tailor having finished fitting out a dinner jacket for one of his customers; walked up to Mohsin to learn their purpose.

Having been introduced by Mohsin and the requirements spelt out; the tailor commenced with his measurements. Simultaneously he also chatted with Akram; with the characteristic ease of all good tailors (and butchers and barbers and car mechanics). He asked him about the climate in India, the *biryani*[19] of Hyderabad (he knew it you bet), how people lived there, what they did, and all that and more. Having measured Akram out

[19] A popular Indian dish where the mutton and rice are cooked together

for the coat; the old tailor now came down to noting the statistics for his trousers. He first noted down his waist, followed by the circumference at his hip level, the width of his thighs, the narrowness at the ankles and the length up to where the trouser must fall. He then looked up at Akram and asked him if he as yet had been on the London Eye or the Grosvenor Bridge. Even as Akram answered, the tailor opened out his tape to measure the seat; that is, the extent from the waist (from the position of the belt buckle) – downwards between the thighs (just below where the zipper ended) – and up again to the rear (to a little above the tail bone and till the height of the belt).

And then with the conversation having died down and the silence bearing heavy, the tailor peered up (from above his pince-nez glasses) at Akram and asked, "So Sir, how do you park?"

Akram (finding the question rather vague and entirely out of context) : "What?"

Tailor : "I mean, Sir, where do you park?" (Smilingly)

Akram (having seemingly understood and gaining in confidence) : "Oh! Wherever I find the place to do so, or wherever it can be easily parked. In India there's plenty of space - and even while some parking's are tight, most are still quite broad and open; definitely not as narrow or at such exorbitant parking charges as in London. And then in Hyderabad where I live, majority parking's are still free. But yes, Delhi today has these multi storied buildings, where they park on all floors".

Tailor (now with a mischievous look in his eyes) : "Sir, that's all very fine. But since I have to allow some space, I specifically would like to know – as to which side do you park? That is; to the left, right, upwards or tucked under?"

Akram : (Looking out of the window, to where he had parked. But just in time to be tapped lightly on his shoulder by Mohsin - who so far had been half lost flipping through a glossy fashion magazine).

Mohsin (whispering into Akram's ear) : "What the old fellow wants to know is, how you adjust and tuck in your 'family jewels' into your underwear when you dress up. You know, they commonly ask this question here, whenever they measure you out for a trouser".

Akram (feeling warm under his collar and clearly embarrassed) : "Ah, well I park to the left!"

Tailor : "A law abiding citizen, Sir! I must say". (this time grinning broadly).

And then all three of them heartily laughed together; an honest and un-suppressed laughter.

And this, Akram told Nadim, was the one most memorable incident of his whole trip. That night as Nadim pondered over his own accustomed sense of parking! He wondered if the story Akram narrated was really true.

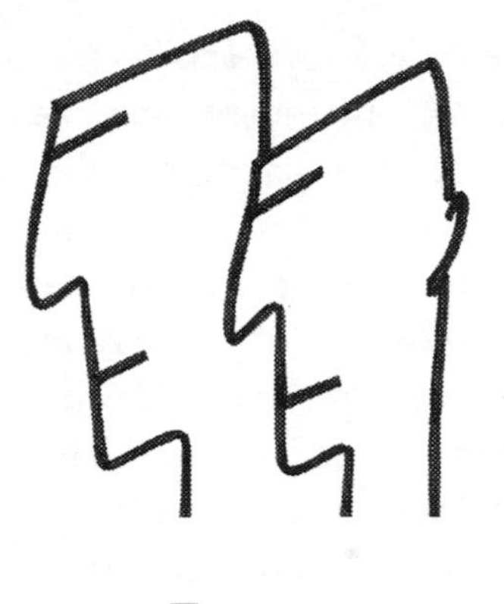

Faces

(Some people read palms and some read the tarot cards. But this guy was different. He had a way with reading faces. And this is what he said of them)

'The world is full of faces. Some people have very calm and quiet faces, just like a placid lake without as much a ripple. Whereas some have faces like on ocean-storm. Some have faces like the clear blue skies; you can not only look at them but through them and see the reflection of their soul, which is also clear and transparent. These are the people whom when you meet you instantly like them. Their sense of peace and quiet slowly starts rubbing on you, and the beauty is you can feel it. These people are like 'saints' in a way, for the positive energy they generate is uncommon. You want to spend more time with them but find yourself unable to do so. But you hope in your heart to meet them again. Without knowing such people in depth, you can anytime vouch for their honesty, simplicity and purity. People like these, let us call them the lake face and the sky face people, they are like pearls in the dark and murky depths of our world, one must never lose them.

Then there are other faces; faces on which cunning, shrewdness, jealousy, egoism, suspicion and doubt are written in block capitals. You must at all cost avoid such people, because you will find that they are in their natural way causing you constant agony, disturbing your mental peace and inspiring similar tendencies in you. These people are like cheap 3 dimensional tickets, whichever ways you look at them you see a different picture. Their faces in fact are like masks, which they change every now and then as per their desire. They often surprise you by wearing a mask which you least expected them to wear on an occasion. Such people are so obsessed with these masks that they keep changing them even at home. Subsequently in life, they are susceptible to getting entangled in their own net of deceit and hypocrisy.

I say to you that each man's face is a mirror which reflects the nature of his soul. Each face you see around you is in fact a story which you can read. Some people have very ambitious faces while some have very contented ones. You know them the moment you see them. The man with the ambitious face may be looking straight at you, but probably he is thinking ahead, as to how he would use you in future or what he could possibly gain out of you. On the other hand, the contented face looks at you and listens to you; it needs nothing from you. If it can, it will help you; if it can't, it won't harm you.

Let us look at the face of a child; it can clearly reveal as to how the child is treated at home. Whether he is having a carefree childhood or his parents have crushed and stifled the child in him. One hard look at a face and you know if the woman is walking a straight line or is sitting on the fence.

A face is nothing but an inner glimpse of a person. And if you look carefully, you can catch the shadows of the thoughts and ideas flashing across the person's mind. So in this hustle of life, if you take a moment and look around, you will see faces of all types. In addition to the lake face, the sky face and the 3D ticket faces which we have already talked of, you might also see the storm face, the swamp face, the sunshine face, the never say die face and the angel face as well. If you see any other types I'm sure you'll let me know.'

The Wind

(I asked him about the wind and he said)

'Have you ever wondered why it blows or from where it comes and where it goes? Does it start from a house or a hole in the ground? And does it, if at all, return home or falls to the floor wherever it is exhausted? Why does it blow and go on blowing endlessly, so it seems? Is it to make music out of our wind-chimes or electricity from our wind-mills?

Does it make waves over water to cheer the sad and gloomy depths of the ocean, or is it some game with the fishes? Does it break into waves on a beach because it is tired of its long voyage, or is to thrill the people on vacation? Does it blow to help eagles soar to the highest of heights, without even flapping a wing? Or is it to push the little amateur birds into the sky, coaxing them to fly? May be it blows to carry the fragrance of flowers to those who are busy 9 to 5 and have no time to smell things other than coffee, hotdogs or their girlfriend's perfumes?

Does it blow to carry the wild pollen to far and distant lands - without a thought to passport, visa or custom clearance? Or does it blow to help women dry their hair after a bath, as they stand on their balconies; knowing how little time they have left for themselves - with all the chores of cooking, cleaning, washing, caring and loving to perform. Or does it blow to help the poor children afford the cheapest pleasure of kite flying? As if knowing how meager their pocket money or earnings are.

Sometimes it blows right into our faces. Is it to smoothen out the tension lines on our foreheads? Or is it a slap of disapproval on the serious ways we lead our funny lives? Whatever it is, she surely is a vagabond - on a ticketless tour around the world; passing over deserts, glaciers, mountains, swamps, ditches, slums and all other complexities of our world. I would grade her as a rather temperamental creature; sometimes calm, sometimes rough, sometimes gentle, and sometimes tough.

Sometimes the way it howls, it seems like an orphan cursing the world; or a passionate soul crying for its lover. Most often however it is quiet and keeps to itself. Though sometimes like a lover, whispering sweet nothings to us or at times like a ghost, banging its fists on our doors and windows.

Finally at the end of the day I find it pushing the boats to the shores, the birds to their nests and the clouds to their valleys. But then despite all this it still keeps on blowing, leaving me wondering as to where it is going?'

Nature

(One day when I asked my students to write a brief note on the marvels of nature, one of the pieces which in particular drew my attention, read)

'The third most important thing which today attracts and has a spell binding effect on us humans is 'nature', the first being sex and the second being money.

There are people who simply feel contented to watch the beautiful marvels of nature and click their cameras; to them nature is just a beautiful sight to see and preserve the images on a camera-roll or a motion film. I feel pity for these people because they only see but fail to listen. When they hold a rose in their hand, they only see the redness of its petals and the sharpness of its thorns; they do not hear what the rose has to tell them. When these people see a sunset, they only see but are unable to listen - what the sun has to say to them in parting.

On the other hand there are a few mad-men like me who find that the loudest voice which reaches them above all the confusion and chaos of life is that of nature. When

I found myself alone in the forest one day, each tree was eager to tell me a tale. The hard and silent looking rocks too had their own private stories to share. The dry leaves and twigs on the forest floor have always shared their secrets with me as I have passed over them. A shy looking wild flower blushed itself pink in telling me how it had been witness to the love-making of two bees one summer afternoon.

Somehow I feel that my conversations with nature are always best when I'm alone. Like when I see a sunset all by myself and find the sun sharing all its feelings with me. The red rose, the gulmohar tree, the greenest grass, the brownest mud, the darkest night and the brightest stars have all spoken to me one time or the other. What each of them said is a separate story in itself. Like the mountains have told me of the joys which lie in achieving great heights, the lakes have told me what depths lie beneath still waters and the sky which told me how small a part I was of the whole cosmos.

You wouldn't believe me if I told you what the wind whispered to me yesterday or what the bougainvillea bush has said to me this morning. One day the neem tree shared its sorrow with me, and the *tulsi*[20] plant which my grandmother has been watering for years is the most talkative ever tulsi I've seen; it knows more about my grandmother than me.

The lake was very pensive yesterday; it said that lately the fishermen were killing far too many fish and that this wasn't just right. I guess the way the lake was feeling it might drown a few fishermen very soon. The mango tree too while showing me the small green and bright mangoes

---

[20] A plant with religious significance for the Hindus

sprouting on its branches, told me that they were going to be twice as sweet as in the last season, but that it was annoyed at the little boys who kept pelting stones at it each afternoon.

The old trees along the highway have been quite sad in telling me how ignored and unwanted they feel; they said that despite the people passing by so often, no one remembers them and no one cares.

I guess all around us nature longs to speak to us, but most of us are just too busy or just too lost in the noises of our individual lives. And without hearing what it wants to say, we have reduced nature to just another painting or a picture postcard.'

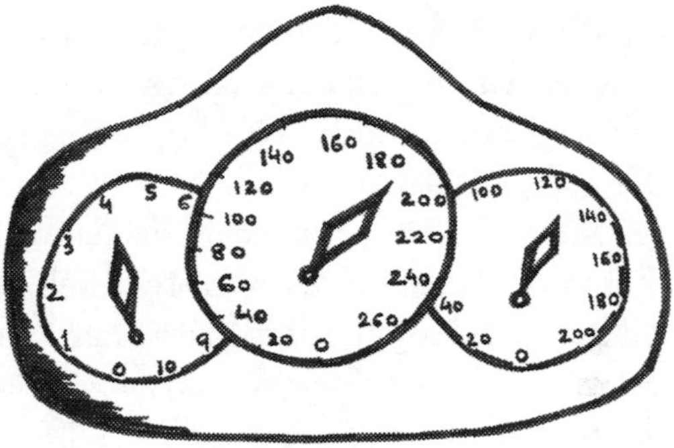

183 Mph

Rocky by nature was not someone whom you could call rash. He was rather a careful sort of a fellow. He liked to take care of things as much as he could and comply with the safety instructions where ever applicable; may it be seat belts, child locks, fire alarms, antivirus software, non-skid shoes, passwords or whatever. Taking unnecessary risks or living recklessly was not his nature. He ate oats even when no one was watching and he could easily eat a pizza. He avoided hard liquor and carbonated drinks. Instead of burgers he snacked on nuts; he had read that they were rich in anti-oxidants. He never partied late. Getting up early and going for a jog had been a habit of years. And although being a cycling enthusiast, he disliked speed cycling and had taken to all terrain biking on week-ends. He never rode without his helmet and always looked twice before crossing the street. He didn't bungee jump on his college vacation either. After school he did his engineering and that with the highest academic grades possible. While others boozed or chased girls, he played his guitar and painted on weekends. Then he got picked-up in a campus interview and now headed a research team in a leading multinational. He was doing well and steadily making his way up the corporate ladder; throughout remaining true to his slow and calm nature.

Then he married a girl seven years his senior. She was in fact his boss and both balanced each other well. She loved a fast paced life - working hard, partying hard, drinking, dancing, pub hopping, throwing parties on weekends etc.; while Rocky remained his laid back usual self - listening country music, reading, painting and idling whenever given an opportunity. They gelled well and in the next five years had two beautiful children, a viable proof of a well consummated marriage. Rocky for a long time efficiently managed it all; balancing his job, wife, kids, ageing parents, finances, vacations, middle age etc. But slowly it became exceedingly packed and hectic. He had no idea of how his days and months passed unnoticed. There was no time with him – either for himself or for leisure. It reminded him of the circus, where a dog continuously ran to stay upright on a spinning ball. The only time he now had for himself was while driving to and back from his work every day. It was here that he found his space; that he could just ponder, or think, or muse or do a reality check or whatever – which was so much a part of his nature.

Then one day he bought himself an eight cylinder 375 horsepower machine; a hurricane of a car, with a top speed of 183 mph. It was the latest model of the Ferrari. The F355 Spider, a limited edition Bond car (the one driven by Xenia Onatopp when racing 007 on the road towards Monte Carlo in the 'GoldenEye'). This car could leave the wind behind and made every other automobile on the road look like a bullock-cart or a horse-drawn buggy. Anyone who saw or heard of his car and had ever known Rocky (for any length of time) were taken by surprise and sat-up. The F355 Spider and Rocky didn't fit together. Something seemed to be coming. Something was surely out of frame.

It was a thirty mile drive from his home to the office (one way). And Rocky always took the Golden Glade Road (that is the sea link) which ran its entire length over the sea. So every day while he drove he could see the waves crashing all along the thirty mile stretch; fishing trawlers chugging along and the sea gulls diving for a catch and letting out their high pitched screeching cries. While the link was a slow moving traffic serpent in the morning; at night however, every day as he left his office, the road was generally unused - all six lanes open to him and inviting a run as Rocky returned.

Today had been a long day and despite that there was much left to be done; but for now he called it off. It was 9 pm and he knew they waited for him. On reaching back they were to rush to a pool side dance party. Tomorrow was his mother's second cataract surgery and his children's school annual day too. The tax returns needed to be filed urgently along with the company insurance premiums. The day after that, they were hosting a barbecue party. And over the weekend he was to accompany his wife to the Dubai shopping festival. Try as he might but he couldn't remember the last time that he had strummed his guitar or picked up a book. But this is how life was. And for now he didn't want to think of any of it.

As he stepped out of his office building, a light breeze came in from the sea and the car reflected a dull red (the color of blood). Under the starlit sky the Ferrari looked beautiful. But also a bit menacing - like a phantom of the night; a machine that was its own master. As he walked to the car park Rocky felt happy; he was again on loose gravel which slipped under his leather soled shoes, as he strode briskly with a satchel in his hand. The gravel was tricky; the faster you walked, the faster it would slip and lesser the distance you covered. With having to walk across the patch twice every day, Rocky knew just the right pace at which to draw maximum distance and pleasure out of it. The feel and the crunching sound of the slipping gravel and the little sense of imbalance that it suggested always worked on him and lifted his mood. It allowed him a strange disconnect from the world and helped him stabilize; a secret which only he or the gravel knew.

Even as he settled into the driver's seat and fastened his seat belt; he could sense the untamed power coiled deep in the engine's belly. All set to hit the sea link, Rocky fired the engine and stepped on the gas. It was like releasing the hold on a thousand wild stallions. He now revved on a deserted six lane runway. There was no one else here today; just him, his F355 Spider and a good life going. Making a mockery of the distance the car cut through the night. And soon they were already at the point where the sea link curved sharply as it aligned itself and turned inland. Rocky loved this stretch. It reminded him of the Grand Prix where the cars overtook one another and burnt their rubber on the turns. This section always gave him a kind of a zero gravity experience and a tickling in the groin. Entering the bend at a rapid pace and then steadily accelerating till you exit the loop, was a constant temptation. The engine begged for gas and speed was a liberating experience. Entering 'Casablanca' (what Rocky had nicknamed the loop) he placed his foot on the accelerator pedal and sharpened his concentration. Turning well through the initial curve he was now on the sharper section leading inland.

And then just like that, without any premonition it started going all out of control; all too very fast. Things around were slipping. Rocky couldn't make out much very clearly. Everything seemed a blur. There was no time to take a grip on things; not even enough to see them go by. This was dangerous. Nothing he tried mattered. The speed was its own devil. He knew it was too late. It was unfair, but the game was up.

He was just in his mid-forties; with so much more to see and so much yet to come. This was not what he had ever imagined would be. Or not something that he had known or wanted. A slowly lived life and now all lost to speed; was this he himself or was it happening to someone else?

While his Ferrari cruised safely at the usual 40 miles per hour (that was just as fast as Rocky ever went) his 'life' was hurtling ahead at a nerve wrecking pace - speeding away, all out of control and beyond his grasp, at 183 miles per hour.

A Flight of Fancy

The plane taxied for a while then turned and aligned its nose to the runway. At first it moved slowly, then catching speed it finally took off. Since he had requested a window seat, Firoz was obliged to look outside. He peered down below. Traffic was plying the roads. Everyone was in the usual hurry. He saw the scooters, cars, buses and trucks and even the small shacks along the road. Now he passed over the houses, their roof tops, big gardens, vast lawns, private swimming pools, the multi-storied flats and other concrete towers. Then steadily gaining height, he saw the still vacant and empty spaces within the city; which he thought never existed and were perhaps yet to be discovered by the men down below. All these grew smaller, shrinking away, and now he saw vast stretches of unclaimed land (making him wonder as to how little of the earth man really possessed) - appearing as pieces of brown and pieces of green; stitched together like a patch-work quilt - the work of a master artisan. The roads were still discernible, stretching like hardened arteries along the parched skin of our old land. Then slowly and steadily the houses, cities, rivers and real estate all vanished and went out of view; till they couldn't be made out anymore. Was all of that really there down below? Or was it only him, who just thought so? And then going deeper he was swallowed by the azure blue skies. Below lay the clouds and the world which he had thought so real; now exceedingly vague and insignificant. You could hardly see it through the clouds anymore. In a matter of minutes he had got away from it all. How fragile were the concerns and trappings of our mind? How surreal was our world? How intangible our existence? Firoz hated to think so much. He closed his eyes and shut out all the voices in his head. He wanted to rest his mind. But then one voice rose above them all - a soft female voice, gently asking 'Sir, what meal would you prefer, vegetarian or non-vegetarian?'

A Mirror

(Life was busy and things moved fast. One smiled, cried, laughed and lived only as was expected of him. Slowly it seemed, one had lost all means to know how one truly and deeply felt within. Honest feelings were rare to come by. As he heard us talking, the old gardener smiled – even while it wasn't expected of him and said)

'If you want to know how you really feel about the way your life is going, or if you are really happy or sad or excited or nervous or whatever parameter you want to measure of yourself, you simply have to do one thing - look at the manifestations of nature. Just look around you. Look at the sky, lake, trees, grass, bushes, flowers or whatever element of nature is around you and check the feelings which any of these inspires in your heart.

If you are happy within yourself, the same is reflected to you by nature which surrounds you; and likewise if you are sad. The small *ashoka*[21] tree; about three feet in height

[21] A common garden tree in India

and growing up outside my window, appeared to be very lonely, miserable and bored with its destiny - simply rooted to the ground, unable to see places, burning itself in the sun and being just a small tree. This - when I was feeling sad and miserable myself. However the same young tree, when I was happy within - appeared to be abounding in total joy; its leaves shining bright, full of the green colour of life. It seemed determined to grow to a really tall height, as if destined to be the tallest tree in the garden. It was dancing in the breeze and seemed the most promising young tree to me.

When I was gloomy, the huge lake appeared to me to be dying a slow death of melancholy. It was still like a corpse, not an odd wave over it and it looked scary and full of poison. But when I was happy, the same dead lake appeared to me - as if it would burst up into the sky any instant. It looked like a child, outwardly sober but its mind bursting with all wild plans of mischief and careless fun. The same gloomy black water looked like mercury; glistening brightly in the sun and ready to scatter into a million shinning droplets, if lifted out of the lake.

When I am happy, the breeze seems crazy and upbeat, but when I am sad; the same breeze seems a nuisance. No matter how skillfully you hide your true feelings from everyone; or even put on a happy or sad face to fool yourself while looking in the mirror, but then, when you look at the ashoka tree or the lake or the sky or the stars or any other element of nature – you find your true feelings standing naked in your mind's eye.'

Sunshine

(From the diary of a soldier who served far away from the comforts of his home)

'It was on this particular day in November, when it was rather cold and chilly and the sky was overcast, that in the rush of things I forgot to put on my jacket while going out with my Company - for the day's work in the field. Our job involved guarding a stretch of road which was particularly prone to being planted with IED's (that is Improvised Explosive Devices) and was a favourite stretch with the terrorists for springing an ambush and blowing up army trucks. We started the day at three in the morning - using all possible means, such as metal detectors, sniffer dogs, electronic jammers, radio frequency generating equipment and our eyes and ears to locate any hidden mines or explosives. We physically searched the entire stretch of the road (about fifteen kilometers) for any bombs or booby traps; and then also the areas astride the axis; that is up to a depth of about 500 meters on either side. Daily starting at about 3 am; it would be by morning nine that we generally finished sanitizing the area. I would then pass a radio message to my headquarters, which would be the green signal for the long military convoys to start rolling out.

It undoubtedly remained very monotonous and boring stuff for us to do – day after day; and terribly stressful too, as you risked yourself being blown up or shot by the likes of crazy goons as *Hizbul Mujahedeen, Jaish-e-Mohammed, Lashkar-e-Toiba*[22] etc (and believe me the list is really endless). There was however a greater weight of responsibility on us; which was the knowledge that if you didn't carry-out your job meticulously, you would be jeopardizing the lives of hundreds of soldiers (mostly either going home to their families or returning from leave), who would be travelling in those military buses that day. Though one didn't know any of them personally; but then there is not much to know in a soldier (any one is the same as the other - like potatoes in a sack). And then once the search was over and just before the long string of military vehicles was to pass, we would take up our positions (in groups of three to four soldiers) on certain pre-identified dominating features astride the axis – to allow the convoy to pass through safely.

It is just as we had so settled into our tactical positions that day (in the thick of winters in Kashmir), that the wind started with a merciless fury and the biting cold seemed to double with every passing moment. Soon my fingers went numb and the cold began to make me miserable. To sit down on the hard rocks meant feeling even colder; so I just stood there shuffling on my feet and trying to keep my fingers and toes from freezing. I was sullen and cursing

22 Some of the terrorist groups operating in the state of Jammu & Kashmir

myself, as I had forgotten to put on my jacket that day in a hurry. Almost all others seemed comfortable in their heavy coats and surely not as stuck up as me.

Finally, feeling awfully cold and tired I sat down on a boulder. Just about the same time, to make matters worse - a sudden and rude drizzle began to fall from the dull grey sky. Now not only feeling cold but starting to get wet as well, I was dead sure of a rotten and long day ahead (our duty would end only when the last vehicle had passed through, generally by about 5 pm). Just then, as I had closed my eyes for a moment to brace myself, a sudden warm feeling came over me; opening my eyes I found that despite the drizzle, sunshine was bursting through the clouds. I thanked the sunshine and the sun for being there and for breaking through the grey clouds that day and soon the drizzle stopped too.

It seemed strange as to how the sun had unexpectedly emerged (as if reading my thoughts). The weather was now wet but warm – on the whole, more conducive to life. I will not say that it turned out to be a bright and sunny day; but surely, for the balance of the day the sun fought bravely with the clouds and came around every now and then, shining with full vigour. Thus overall I remained more dry than wet, more warm then cold and surely not as miserable as I had initially started out to be.

I guess it's time for us to thank the sun for all the times that it has come around, through the clouds and the rain, and kept us warm – knowing perhaps how vulnerable we are to feeling gloomy and forgetting our jackets in the rush of our daily lives.'

A Strange Sensation

A.H. Nadiawala that is Akbar Hassan Nadiawala (alias Hassan) was a serious man. No one had ever seen him laugh or to even smile faintly. Jokes fell on him like water on a duck's back. If his grandchildren ever dared to tickle him in the armpits, or at the sides of his belly or on the soles of his feet; he only got scratches or redness from all the poking and nothing more or nothing less. He was a Senior Manager in the city branch of the Urban Cooperative Bank and simultaneously moonlighted as a Tax Consultant for small and medium enterprises. Overall an important man, with the right amount of seriousness to handle accounts and insipid financial transactions.

Now if you happened to ever see him walking down the street, you couldn't miss him even if you were blind. He was the tall type - a few notches over six feet and an impressive ram-rod bearing. Hassan was neither thin, nor fat, nor exceptionally muscular either; but just the right amount of weight that makes a man appear healthy and gay (gay - as in happy, and not as in *LGBT*[23]). But since this would fit the general description for quite a lot of men walking down the street, you mustn't care to focus this aspect too keenly. What instead you should look out for, is a man wearing a dark coloured *Safari Suit*[24]. And with that his peculiarities; the shirt with four pockets and a soldier's shoulder lapels (always and every time), the trouser with four front pleats (always) and the shoes (each time) of the oxford pattern (handmade and of patent black leather). On his left hand, he wears a heavy Rado wrist watch on a black metal strap. On his right hand, he wears a magnetic wrist strap (made up of small rectangular magnets and believed to keep the blood pressure under control).

His head is of the distinct shape of that of an old time baboon (of the ape family) – where the face appears sharply angular; that is each feature of the face running a step ahead of the other. Say if you started at his forehead, the eyebrows were a step ahead, the nose was further forward, and then was the upper lip, which was defeated by the lower lip – which in turn, was led by the chin. In fact his long-drawn-out chin made one wonder if the doctor had perhaps pulled him out from his cubby hole (wherefrom the young Hassan had no intention to emerge) - by clasping his forceps around it. On his nose always rests gold rimmed spectacles, which of course has no risk of slipping (given the angular length of his face). On his head is a heavy bush of hair; which towards the nape of his neck, almost entirely covers the shirt collar and on the very top (that is at the crown of his head) is buoyant and blooms sprightly – falling

---

23 Acronym for Lesbian-Gay-Bisexual-Transgender

24 A suit wherein the shirt and the trouser are both of the same colour and fabric

equally on all sides, like a bunch of innocent gladioli. It in fact lends his head the semblance of an overgrown fern in a clay pot, or a sparrow - when it swells its chest out and fluffs up all its feathers. Even though Hassan is fast nearing the retirement age, the plumage on his head is predominantly black; with only the lower portions of the strands, defiantly silver – indicating a ripening of the mustard. And least I forget to mention - he always keeps a smooth upper lip and a thick French beard.

Even though leading a reasonably busy life, he had always given great attention to his health. He never let even a small itch, or a rash, go un-honoured. He would find time, somehow or the other and consult a physician – and buy and apply, whatever lotion or cream was medically prescribed. He still was stronger than his sons and could toss his grandchildren into the air. It was all a result of paying close attention to the signals given by one's body. If he had a noisy or a windy stomach, he would follow a two day diet of fruits. If it was a sore throat, he would chew on ginger and avoid ice creams and colas for a month. However in the course of the last few years – as he ran his sixtieth lap – Hassan along the way had tinkered with arthritis, diabetes, prostrate disorder and kidney stones. But it was all his timely and early attention, and the fanatical zeal in implementing the doctor's orders that he had overtaken them all; and with a few – he was still giving them the run of their lives. Hassan besides going in for only allopathic drugs had a concurrent faith in homeopathy and herbal medicine too. Even when healthy, he was on an average having six or seven tablets a day (for this or for that). The end result was a ruddy complexion, an enduring appetite and an effervescent disposition.

Hassan amongst his friends was known for his love of fine clothes and tasteful dressing. In pursuing this passion, he always favoured finesse and class. Money was no rider when it came to dressing up. He bought only the best. In fact all his added income from the part time tax consultancy that he did was exclusively set aside for finer indulgences in life; such as branded apparel, flavoured tobacco, exquisite colognes or an occasional spa. His shirts were all an imported label. So were his trousers. His shoes were handmade by the best craftsman in the city. Similarly, his suits were all upmarket and fashioned at the most exclusive outlets. And even for the handkerchief, underwear, vests and socks – he never bought them off the street side shacks (where they sold a dime a dozen), they had to be branded too. He had his own preferred shops – which sold only in undergarments and offered the best of the imported brands. Call it his only fetish, but so it was. Getting value for money, he patronized the same shops over the years with dogged loyalty. Thus he was a recognized and remembered customer, whenever or wherever he shopped. His measurements were not only entered in leather bound registers at the tailors, shoemakers etc. but were by and large recalled by memory, by most of the salespersons at his favoured haunts. Like the other day when he went in to get measured for a *'Sherwani*[25]*'*, the old tailor had remarked - "Hassan Sahib, you seemed to have thinned a little at your wrists". Such show of exclusivity and recall always lifted his spirits. In fact the shop keeper at his old tobacco shop even called him up each time they received his favourite flavours.

[25] A long coat running up to the knees and worn with a trouser narrowing sharply at the ankles

The last two years had however taken an unexpected and heavy toll on Hassan. May be it was the increased work load in his new section, or the driving through the ever increasing traffic every day, or the small things which needed to be taken care of all the time at home (i.e. leaking taps, electricity bills, cooking gas etc.); or perhaps the combined effect of all of these. But it couldn't exactly be said with certainty, as to what it was, that had led to Hassan's recurring bouts of splitting headaches and the endless sensation of loud bells ringing in his ears (which almost cost him his sanity) accompanied by deep palpitation and sweating in the palms. In office he would now get irritable, fidgety and extremely uneasy towards the evenings (with the continuous clamour of bells in his ears). And at night, he often broke a cold sweat and had soul jarring nightmares.

His appetite suffered a steady decline and his old vigor too, was slowly ebbing away. Try as they might, the physicians couldn't put their finger on any conclusive diagnosis. It was now months of endless medication. And doctors began to play their favourite game of elimination of probabilities. So followed endless experiments – wherein one by one they hit each symptom (howsoever faint or farfetched) with the heaviest of drugs. Thus hoping, to finally be left with the one incurable illness, to which the battered life of our friend could be solemnly surrendered. While was ruled out one disease after the other, the case got only worse. It was in the doctor's opinion, an unprecedented combination of life threatening symptoms; a strange malady – nowhere documented in the annals of medical history. Apparently (as doctors in their profession cannot afford to appear naive), it was ascribed as an onset of Alzheimer's and dementia, accompanied by early neurosis and advanced liver malfunction. Heavy drugs now flowed through Hassan's vessels. Mild medicines were first substituted by strong antibiotics and then succeeded by modern day steroids. But all to no avail. Our brother's life was now at stake. His blood had grown thick and shamefully saturated with all the known medicines in the world. To the extent, that just a drop of it, could now cure the most deviously rampant diseases in man or beast. But nothing helped Hassan himself. The jarring sounds and the soul wrenching clamour of bells in his ears had aggravated his tremors and palpitations; and had rendered the man lamentable and listless. The brain having become victim to a vile sabotage, the body grew weak day by day. Akbar Hassan Nadiawala, our old friend, was now running a very close race. He appeared as if imprisoned and stifled by an invisible foe. It seemed to him that somewhere within; an unknown enemy had already dug in his claws and steadily smothered his life. He had long lost the interest in clothes, accessories and life in general. While Hassan had earlier been somewhat of an atheist (you may say), but failing health had now made him to turn towards religion and spirituality. Giving up his daily two smalls of scotch and half a plate of mutton kebabs, he now felt closer to God. Every morning and night he would say his prayers fervently and also chanted on the holy beads. His family concurrently undertook pilgrimage to all known houses of worship and made offerings for restoring of his mental peace and vitality. Of course nothing helped. When a man's time has come, it is simply inescapable. Anyway, the family has a force of its own and undaunted by lack of improvement, they kept up their efforts.

Battling ill health for the last over two years; things really looked low and our friend was on the verge of a total collapse. His decision to seek a Voluntary Retirement – was the thought uppermost in his mind, as he locked his office cabin this evening. Perhaps he would let his family know of it tonight itself after dinner. But for now, he needed every remaining fragment of energy in his body to cover the short distance home. Crossing the busy town square, which earlier had always excited Hassan – was now merely a matter of routine. The ailing man had lost complete interest in his erstwhile passions. So far as he remembered, except for his medicines he hadn't bought a thing in the last two years; not even a tie-pin. As he crossed the street it was beginning to get dark. He noticed a bright neon sign board being put up at a shop front and sales advertisements on its window panes. He paused with a sense of déjà vu and then suddenly remembered that this was his very own shop - where he had always bought his thermals, vests and underpants. It had been quite a while that he had last been there – may be over two years. But today he entered not by premeditation, but simply drawn in by the brightness of the new neon board. And then he remembered that he needed to buy some underpants as well. The shop was crowded with customers. It seemed like a clearance sale. How people these days could literally be sold anything, anything – even poison; if only you could make it look a little fashionable he thought. But this of course was only a sale of men's underpants and nothing life threatening. The old shop owner (almost the same age as Hassan) caught sight of our friend in the crowd and instantly raised a greeting, "Hassan Sahib, *Khushamadeed! itne samay baad*[26]". Heads turned in the crowd and Hassan was delighted to be recognized.

---

[26] What a pleasure! and in such a long time

Well the shop was awfully crowded with the sales at full pitch; but then the old shop owner was a loyalist. He brushed aside a bunch of first time customers, allowing Hassan to close in at the counter. The owner then asked our friend - Where he had been all this while and how he wondered, if Hassan had been transferred to some other bank and had moved out of town. Akbar Hassan Nadiawala on his part congratulated him for the ongoing facelift of the shop and then told him how he had bought in bulk, in a similar clearance sale at his shop about two and a half years back; and thus had had no need to return in between. The owner smiled politely and mentioned how he remembered it all. Then he surprised Hassan by showing him their latest stock of Hassan's all-time favourite – '105 centimeter (cms) V shaped cotton briefs' (of course he had remembered) ; which Hassan had always bought until before his last mega purchase.

And then Hassan told him, how he had (since his last visit to the shop) been wearing only '90 cms size' (which he had than bought in bulk) and had gotten used to their tight and snug fit. But then the old shopkeeper still insisted that Hassan buy only the 105 cms size; and how the inexperienced salesman in the shop back then, had probably had no idea as to what size to suggest to different customers. But when Hassan stood adamant at buying only the 90 cms sized underpants (and once again mentioned their snug fitting), the old shopkeeper narrowed his eyes and bending over the counter – waved Hassan to come closer. And then with a sense of camaraderie, whispering into Hassan's ear shared an old secret with him – "Sahib, wearing underpants of the wrong size and that too of such a tight fit as 90 cms, can play havoc with a person's life". And then seeing the quizzical and dazed look on Hassan's face as he asked "What do you mean?"; the shop keeper further added, that "If worn for prolonged periods, a tight fitting underpants such as this, gives rise to a strange sensation of loud bells ringing in one's ears, cold sweating in the palms, frightful dreams at night and recurring headaches. In brief it can rob a man of his peace and vitality. The victim may even be tempted to assume he has probably gone mad, and that, as if his life is slowly slipping away". And then the shop keeper went on to expound as to how buying of underpants is not to be treated with a trifle or carelessly; and how it should not be left to the suggestions of young and inexperienced salespersons. And why the advice of the old and learned (as him), in such matters, must never be brushed aside. And that how his great grandfather, in his time, had once seen a healthy man wasted away and utterly devastated by a blunder such as this.

Hassan's jaw dropped and with the colour suddenly leaving his face, he looked deathly pale and mortified. Staggering, he took support of the newly constructed counter and just about managed to keep himself on his feet. He looked like a man into whose chest a sword had been thrust. Standing close, a few customers thought he would pass out. But then no man passes away before his time has come. Gathering all the shreds of life that were still left in him, Hassan, in a barely audible whimper – asked for a glass of water and instructed the old shop keeper to pack him a dozen of the '105 centimeter sized briefs' right away; and to make it really fast since he was in a raging hurry. Then on an impulse, our friend didn't wait to get home to make the amends, but used the shop's changing room right away.

The old shopkeeper had understood it all and as Hassan was leaving, he bid him a sincere "*Khuda Hafiz*[27]".

Needless to say and unbelievable though it may seem but then the bells ceased to toll and our friend's recovery was both remarkable and unprecedented. The change of underwear had salvaged his life. He was once again back to his usual self and tossing his grandchildren into the air. And of course you wouldn't believe me if I said, how after that, our friend went on to live to a ripe old age of 105 years!

27 May God be with you!

A Beautiful Day

A pair of doves flew together in the sky - not very high above the trees but yet finding their freedom. I watched them from the window of my speeding car. I too was headed the same way. Thus for a short while we (kind of) travelled in tandem; the doves speeding away in the sky above and the car speeding down below. Both almost at the same speeds and headed in the same direction.

They flew with boundless passion and in a spirit of gay abandon. Close together but yet each in his own space. They rose playfully above each other, then dived and teasingly cut across the other's paths; racing, daring and steadily overtaking one another.

Unknowingly, all within their game both had soon gained height. And while I watched them closely to catch a sign of their getting tired; they continued their simple game with unceasing spontaneity and joy.

And now that it had been a while, very soon (I guessed) one of them had to fall behind and then each go his own way. This of course couldn't continue forever. The parting of ways was inevitable and had to happen. But it didn't.

They stayed together. Now the car (in which I travelled) was gaining speed and also taking a curve to the right. The doves were beginning to get a little left behind and their distance from me was increasing. I kept looking back to see if they separated. I watched till as much my neck would turn, but they still didn't split (seemed I had lost a bet to myself). They only kept going together – higher and faster. Till the car turned a bend and I couldn't see them anymore.

Not all journeys are individual and not all associations ephemeral - so I wondered. Smilingly I settled back into the seat. And as I looked out of the window, I suddenly realized that it was a 'beautiful day'.

The Pond at Zazuna

(Firstly 'Zazuna' is a small village in the Sumbal District of Kashmir; secondly, this pond is within the village, and thirdly, I come into the picture because at least once a week for about six months at a stretch my work took me to this village. Sometimes it so happens that you instinctively like a spot where it feels most natural to have a cup of tea or a packed meal. So it was often that I had my tea and packed food sitting at a spot from where this pond lay a short distance away; just adequately far for me not to seem an intruder in the atmosphere of the pond and yet close enough to catch every activity that occurred there. Knowing that you'll never probably be going to Zazuna yourself let me tell you how the things there unfold)

'The day starts with the morning *'Adhan*[28]'; and at about 4:30 am, precisely with the Muezzin's call to Allah, come the first flock of ducks - about ten odd. They get into the

28 Pronounced as - azan; is the Islamic call to worship, recited by the Muezzin at prescribed times of the day

chilly water cackling loudly (or whatever you call the sound of ducks). They tip head down into the cold water, totally upside down (rather downside up!) with bottoms to the sky - they waggle their behinds a few times and then emerge totally dry! (Proving the old adage - advice falling away like water on a duck's back!).

In the second shift, at about 06:30 am come the village girls - about eight to ten of them, in the impressionable age group of fourteen to sixteen years. In between, a few more ducks join in and some leave the pond. These girls come with the dinner utensils of the previous night, scrubbing them clean for the morning tea and breakfast. Once this group leaves, comes the second group of girls - the wise ones who don't to go school; with their clothes to wash. They start washing at about 07:45 am and continue up to 09:30 am. They talk excitedly all the while - they are about eight to ten of them, in the tender age of seventeen to nineteen years. Their gossip comprises primarily about catching up on who's dating who! and similar spicy stuff. And when they are just about getting ready to leave by around 10:00 in the forenoon - with all their dirty clothes washed, arrive the third group of girls - rather young women, about ten to twelve of them in the irresistible age group of twenty to twenty five years. These young women are the ones I find capturing my attention the most; they are really pretty – all-encompassing the legendary beauty of Kashmir. They appear to be returning with the breakfast utensils - scrubbing them clean for the afternoon tea and lunch. By the time they finish, say about 11 am, it is fully bright - the sun having come up nice and warm (the cold fog having slowly and painfully lifted). Now come the ducks again - for their second round of dip and swim session, simultaneously a group of school children trudge their way to school. They pass by the pond chucking stones to scare the ducks and splash water to tease the girls at the pond.

All this activity is then followed by a brief lull, when the pond seems to slip smoothly into its own solitude. Then at about three in the noon, almost simultaneously – arrive two groups of girls; one with the lunch utensils and the other with the tea samovars. Cleaning them yet again for the evening tea and dinner (how we humans require so much to eat!). Also at this time a few men gather near the masjid gate to smoke a hookah. And the school children by now are starting to return cheerfully back from school. A few of these young boys, five to six year olds – throw their school bags aside, peel away their school uniforms and dive into the pond for a swim (by now the sun has killed the chill and warmed the water).

It surprises me that though the pond is quite shallow; these boys know the precise spot where they can dive safely. While the pretty girls wash their utensils, a few teenage boys come to watch the girls. They don't come to the edge of the pond but stay about 20 - 25 meters away, crowding near the old walnut tree at the edge of the graveyard. While the girls are washing, they know that the boys are watching - and so there is a hushed silence amongst them; broken occasionally by some keen whispering and giggling among the girls.

This time of the evening gets to be my favorite time at the pond. The activity and chatter has slowly reached a threshold, like building up of a crescendo in an orchestra. There are children bathing, girls washing, boys watching and so much more. Then join in the ducks once more and a farmer who almost religiously washes his buffalo at about five pm on the far edge of the pond. A few stray dogs come up too; they drink some water and leave quickly. By now it's beginning to be dusk and the sun is slipping away. A few more girls turn up in a hurry to wash their utensils (probably those who have overslept). Once the flurry of activity has subsided and everyone has left the pond, the ducks are still there and they have the last swim of the day. Out of his old habit, the Muezzin from the nearby Masjid makes the day's last call to Allah and with that (so it seems) the ducks leave the water - they remain undoubtedly the first to come and the last to leave.

The water slowly settles down and the pond becomes still once again. In between a few leaves from the nearby old walnut and chinar trees drift down on the water's surface. A stray gust of wind makes a few waves and with the night, the stars and the moon come down to float alongside the chinar and walnut leaves.

There is never a dull moment at the pond at Zazuna.

Yet another dawn and the pond comes to life again. First arrive the ducks.'

Missing

Once upon a time the earth was a thick forest. And while the man lived quietly in his cave, many a splendid creatures freely roamed the wilderness. Back in those days man needed little - only an odd deer, an ibex or a boar once in about ten days. And in the time that remained he either sharpened his axe or painted in his cave. But by and by his needs steadily grew - till they far outdid the rate at which anything else multiplied those days.

And just about this time all the 'Three Winged Falcons' suddenly went missing. Not even one was to be seen anymore. I searched for them day and night. And even though I tediously combed from the high Himalayas in the North to the humid coastal plains in the South; and in-between covering all the deserts, the mangroves and the savannahs - but I found no trace. Neither did anyone even seem to remember as to when they had last been seen.

They were much unlike any of the birds that now remain. Firstly, they had not two - but three wings. And secondly, they didn't fly across the skies - but straight upwards - through and through. That is they descended and took-off vertically; their three wings lifting them up effortlessly - just like the blades of a helicopter. It was a sheer delight to see large flocks of them descend on a tree and then harmoniously take-off heavenwards (that's what the old ones recollected). But now not even one of them remained anymore.

I enquired a great deal but couldn't get any clue. Until, a finch one day asked me the cause of my perplexity - and then said, that her grandfather had long back once told her of the grandeur of the 'Three Winged Falcons' and how all of their lot was now held captive by the tribe of the wild man - who lived in the dark ghettos on the other side of the earth.

Having not home or hearth, or wife or children - I wholeheartedly set myself upon discovering the mysterious fate of the disappeared bird. For years I wandered, but still not reaching the other side of the earth; till perchance I came across this bat, which flew through the man's ghettos by night. He said he would take me with him and show me as to how the birds I searched now lay all trapped.

And that night I saw them for myself. Once the envy of the Gods and the 'Lotus of the Skies' - they were now at the mercy of man. One each of the birds I found tethered to the ceiling in every cubicle of the man's shanty dwelling. Remorselessly strung and fastened by their slender necks. Strangled and gasping for breath, they swirled around in circles - day in and day out. It was heart rending to see them so tortured, endlessly.

As I spoke to them that night, I learnt that though held under the most unfavorable circumstances - the indomitable spirit of the falcon was far from dead. All they waited for was the midnight of the next summer solstice - when the magical breeze from the Blue Mountains was preordained to renew their energies and infuse a new life force into their veins. And then when that happened - together they would shake away the shackles of man and gather in the skies above the ghetto - before rising up through the clouds; hundreds and thousands of them, to meet the spirits of their ancestors. And with the passage of each day and night - the designated hour only draws closer and the hearts of the birds grow more and more impatient with the waiting.

The man meanwhile, unknowing the resolve of the falcon, continues to sleep in the wind they kick up - and mockingly calls them the 'Fans'.

In the Garden

With open spaces and gardens becoming scarcer by the hour, I consider myself really fortunate to have a little backyard and a decent flower patch as well. This may be because I am living in an old government quarter, in a quaint little town in Western India. The occupants before me, as well as the Cantonment Board, have been quite nature friendly in ensuring plenty of greenery and a variety of trees in the surroundings. It is even a greater treat in the monsoons; when after a shower everything is washed clean and a bright green outside. This rejuvenates the vision and soothes the eyes as well (in fact it permanently cured a congenital retinal disorder in an old aunt of mine - so we would both like to believe).

The trees when they grow anywhere draw a variety of birds and all kinds of creatures without fail. So it was natural that my garden too was frequented by both winged and non-winged fauna. Being not an idiot box addict, but only a lazy and laid back onlooker of others; I would often make myself a hot cup of tea and occupy the easy chair next to the window - to simply gaze outside. And so I watched them as they visited.

The Pigeons

Initially they came to pick on the corn and the bread crumbs which my wife put out for them every morning as a ritual. And along with the corn, she also regularly filled out water in a broad and shallow earthen dish for them. So, with one's daily bread so religiously taken care of - the pigeons soon became regular visitors, and then gaining courage they permanently set up home in our bathroom window. They (shamelessly) wouldn't look the other way even when you happened to be bathing. And if you tapped on the glass, trying to shoo them away - they simply stood up, fluffed their feathers, blinked a couple of times and then immediately settled down once again. So from visitors, they became unyielding tenants.

Their deep throated humming soon combined with the sounds of the water cooler to produce a siesta inducing symphony every afternoon. We saw them very closely (with just a thin glass pane between us) - sleeping, laying eggs, mounting each other's backs etc. They stayed so long, that we even saw the young ones grow up and fly away; perhaps to find their very own bathroom window somewhere.

The Babblers

They don't stay very long in the garden. They come in like the storm and go away like the hurricane. Always rushing and in a hurry. They look all alike, like perfect clones of one agitated ancestor. They strike upon my backyard in a group of about nine or ten of them (perhaps from the neighbor's house; but I am not too sure). They are to be seen first on the boundary fence (which is primarily a chain link fence covered by a cloth partition screen). They all sit side-by-side along the fence, leaving exactly one arm distance between each other (like well-disciplined students in a school assembly). But then that's the only discipline to be ever seen in my garden.

For some time (but only a short while) they sit quietly and contemplatively, enjoying the first rays of the morning sun. Then from the fence, they rush down upon the gooseberry bush. And that is almost always where their argument starts. It seems to begin with just a little disagreement; but then the babblers (even though sticking together) never seem to agree on any issue ever. Out of all of them, only two to three are involved in the initial discord. But then one by one, taking sides - they all get drawn in. The argument picks up and suddenly they all rush from the gooseberry bush to the jacaranda tree. The argument continues in the jacaranda tree too. Then they try out all the different branches, each time with a new sitting arrangement, but it doesn't help one bit in settling their differences.

And then the next minute, you find them having descended down to the radish patch. The argument's become pretty loud by now and in fact a bit of chasing is taking place as well. They shuttle and chase each other between the radishes. Cursing, calling, taunting and occasionally pecking each other from behind. From the radish patch they suddenly bolt into the bougainvillea bush; from there on - to the tamarind tree and back to the jacaranda. They are miserably loud and rude to each other all this while. And in similar style the argument continues unabated; even with their changing the trees in such quick succession. Having thus explored the garden, they return to the boundary fence once more. And then without any forewarning, they suddenly take off for the children's park; only to return the next morning with a fresh argument.

The Mynahs

The Mynahs are very quiet and dignified. Once they have flown in into my backyard - they study the clothes that I have washed up that day and put out on the clothes line to dry. Then very deliberately and with no apparent hurry, they tip toe gracefully to where the bread crumbs are scattered; and peck away slowly - taking their time. They are never greedy or hurried in consuming their meal. Even while having their fill of water the Mynahs are equally graceful and controlled. They never make much noise - except for their occasional tweets and the scanty conversation which they make amongst themselves. Also they often puff out their feathers and close their eyes; which I think is a kind of a deep breathing exercise that they follow to keep good health. They however are a fashionable lot; with all of them having a permanent yellow mascara around their eyes - which gives them a unique charm of their own.

One day there came a Mynah, which while everything else about it was perfectly normal - had an almost bald head. All the feathers there had been plucked out; perhaps a bad haircut or the ramifications of an ugly fight. Slowly over the days that followed, the feathers grew back on the Mynah's head and then sadly I couldn't set it apart from the others anymore.

On the whole, they are decent and well-bred visitors; always maintaining a cordial decorum in my garden.

The Doves

They are the shy ones and appear to be quiet and introvert by nature. They don't rush into the garden or make any noise. Neither do they like loud company. They perch high, on the branches of the one and only eucalyptus; which grows at an impossible angle in the south west corner of my backyard (the slant is about five times more than that of the leaning tower of Pisa; it's a miracle how it stays up there). This eucalyptus is old and almost dead and even the distant branches are all dried up - bare and devoid of any leaves or bark; and that is surprisingly where the Doves like to roost. They just sit there quietly - with their occasional deep throated calls. Sitting high above, they silently witness the sundry goings-on down below. In fact they couldn't care less for what really happens under; and are in a way detached. They never venture close to eat the bread crumbs or the corn. And because I have never ever seen them pecking at, or eating anything in my garden, I wonder how they sustain?

While most of them are an even shade of fawn, some are spotted with faint white specks just below the throat. But one day, I guess it was during the monsoons, that a most unusual site presented itself. There suddenly appeared a flock of light green Doves (with a most delicate and soft plumage) - perched high on the dying eucalyptus; finding no way that they could have gathered the hue - I suspect they might have been rolling in the grass for a while. I saw them a couple of times more during the monsoons, and then the brown ones returned. But never did I see the two types together at the same time on the same tree. Whether they were the same set of Doves, simply changing colors; or two different teams - remains an unsolved mystery.

The Peacocks

They are undoubtedly the Airbus Boeing 707 amongst my flying friends. They are large and heavy and with a long tail of colorful feathers. And just like a large plane which needs to gain momentum before take-off; the Peacocks too run and build up a drag before getting airborne. It is strenuous for them to fly given their relatively heavier bulk. They have to flap heavily and do so with all their might, whenever the need arises.

We have a pair which often arrives and strides all over the garden - inquisitive and inspecting all that grows there. They step gingerly between the plants with their long legs. The bread crumbs, corn or any other food offered to them - doesn't much draw their interest; they only love the freshly sowed seeds and the young saplings. Digging out the earth with their strong legs, they easily pick out the planted seeds and savor them like an old connoisseur (in fact it was for this reason that we long wondered and even argued with our gardener – as to why none of the seeds that he planted – ever did sprout).

Their plaintive cry, sounds like the pleading call of a lost lover. The males are beautiful with their rich colorful feathers; while the peahens are austere and always trailing the males. Their beauty and grace can be seen in the way they slowly stretch their necks and turn their heads around (to catch any faint sound or the hint of a movement). They gradually become used to your presence in the garden (as long as you stay still), but even then, keep you under constant watch from the corner of their eyes. Any sudden movement on your part startles them and taking a few swift strides, they lift off with their heavy flapping. In fact

I once thought that a ceiling fan was flying overhead; so strong were their wing beats.

Even though heavy, some sportingly inclined or athletic of them can lift themselves to surprisingly steep heights - I have once seen a pair resting high on the banyan tree in the central park; and then one day, another one, sitting atop the towering water tank of our housing society. And of course there can be nothing more absorbing then their mating dance during the monsoons - the colors are simply too overwhelming and enticing.

The Langurs

They are the real devils and a big nuisance (quite literally) whenever they arrive. Firstly, they are almost as large as me and ten times stronger (to say the least). Secondly, they raid on me in the company of their siblings, children and other relatives (and sometimes their neighbors as well) (here I am reminded of another interesting incident concerning the Langurs; but we will keep it for later, so as not to mix things up). If they don't find ears of corn, tender aborigines, tomatoes or bottle gourd - they as a show of their disappointment can tear down your entire garden in minutes. Worse is, they often make a stinking minefield of my garden - by crapping and pissing all over. And this they don't do squatting down on the ground, but sitting high atop the trees in the garden. I suspect a few of them to be mentally deranged or depressed to be shitting and peeing in the air, from such dizzying heights. They hoot at you and prance around your yard and rooftops without a damn for your privacy or senses. And you still don't dare look them back; cause if they don't like the look in your eyes and happen to take offence, they will simply jump down from the tree - slap you remarkably hard (believe me, it has happened to people) and get back before you can even say Jack (leave aside Robinson).

So, if they raid your garden while you are around outside, all you can simply do is hang your head like a shy new bride and walk in an unhurried pace to your door. Once safely inside, you feel fortunate to not have been slapped and stay-in till the gang is gone. A friend of mine with some jungle survival training, made a strong catapult, and would shoot missiles at the Langur's (aiming for their bare red bottoms) each time they arrived in his garden. But then the brats got the better of him. They identified his car during his goings and coming from the office; and the subsequent Sunday afternoon while he was lazily sipping ginger-lemon tea in his study - they bolted him from outside and descended on his car with sticks and stones; and all the while turning back to look at him. They jumped and danced on his car - before breaking the windshield, the window glasses, the side view mirrors and then getting in and tearing apart the premium leather upholstery; all in his full view. Moreover during all this, three of them, were even clapping and shaking their bare red bottoms at him (so my friend says).

As for me, I don't at all mind the Langurs playing merry-hell in my garden. At least my sedan sits safely in the parking lot across the lawns.

The Bats

The descending night draws out these dark winged creatures into the skies - just as it draws out our darkest desires, fears and fantasies to the surface of our minds. The bigger bats fly silently above, while the smaller ones dart furtively over our heads. The bigger bats are really large and remind one of the legend of the Batman. Seeing their size, I sometimes suspect the stories to be true - and wonder if one amongst those flying above may after all be the elusive Batman himself. The larger ones when viewed against the dark skies; appear to be flying effortlessly, as if in slow motion (with the assurance that even if they flapped twice slower, they wouldn't still fall off the skies). The site even though transfixes you - is far from cheerful and has an ominous air about it. I don't know where they hang themselves during the day? But all the upside down hanging must be giving them a swollen head and a terrible headache all through the night. While I pay close attention and keenly follow their line of flight, I still can't discern their final destination. And during the day, no matter how much I look around, I have never seen them hanging anywhere.

The Woodpeckers

There's a strange family of Woodpeckers in my garden, which have their home in the hollow of the old *goolar tree*[29]. After a week of watching them closely, I concluded that something was amiss and then discovered their strange obsession. In fact I had begun to grow suspicious when I never ever heard them knocking away on wood. Like the other run-of-the-mill woodpeckers they were never to be seen going up and down or around the trees trunks - knocking away with their pick-axe beaks and feasting on the tender termites or the crisp ants.

---

[29] The Indian fig tree

I wonder what they ate to keep themselves going. And that was when I took post and unearthed the whole plot. This couple I discovered - were born again Brahmins. And so, given their brahmnic way of life, they were now turned staunch vegetarians; never to touch a living creature for subsistence. They consumed only berries, fruits, figs, chestnut and sun-flower seeds; and this is what they drew their energy and life force from. They naturally (since you are what you eat) were peace loving and righteous in their conduct; never turning their beaks on one another or any of their winged neighbors. Strange - as to what powers are sometimes unleashed and discipline us (when we fall prey to a fancy doctrine).

They thus continue to live in my garden; leading a healthy and vegetarian way of life.

The Magpie

She is a spinster (so I would like to believe) and is perfectly happy and content to be living alone in her undisturbed bliss. It is not that she has never been in a relationship - that she has seen half a dozen; but now the time for flirting and necking is far behind her (age, if you aren't watchful, can sometimes (very discreetly) rob the fun out of your life). So the Magpie is now given to be quiet, somber and contemplative. She sits on the garden fence each morning, facing away and gazing at the futile strivings of other creatures.

This magpie in her own way is unique; she can sit still for hours at a stretch - without moving a feather or a limb (her standing record being eighteen hours on an empty stomach). Watching with detachment is a therapy, which I suppose works well for her. And then having taken her fill of the meditative silence, she simply flies away; only to be seen with remarkable punctuality the next morning. She twitches her tail whenever she is distracted or getting unwanted attention from some uncouth males. The tail twitching on such occasions is indicative of her growing discomfort and is more often than not followed by her sudden flight.

My son tells me that when you see a single Magpie - you kiss the palm of your hand and whisper 'One for Luck' to yourself. And when you see two of them together - it is 'Two for Joy'. So, while each morning I whisper 'One for Luck'; I am secretly wishing for - a 'Two for Joy' for both the Magpie as well as for myself.

The Cats

They lived on top - one floor above us. In the flat which was un-occupied, dilapidated and awaiting repairs since long. They (i.e. the Cats) lived as indifferently as all good neighbors; amicable only when you happened to be accidently faced with each other on the stairs, in the car park, or in the society lawns. They were a large family. Very much like an undivided Hindu household of yore. Parents, siblings, uncles, aunts and cousins (and sometimes even girlfriends) all muddled together - and getting on each other's nerves. They had slowly moved in and now had the complete three bedroom flat to themselves. Sometimes they fought savagely – (but of course like good neighbors again) - all in the privacy of their home. We would often hear them upstairs - growling, cursing and yelping. The husband was a wife-beater I concluded within a fortnight. They fought in short bursts like a popular soap with commercial breaks in between. One of the Cats even cried like a possessed soul; and generally at about three or four in the morning (the fallout of an unrequited love I later learnt). It was the most dreadful of the things to ever hear in one's life.

They would get down to my garden every morning and return to their apartment only at dusk. Unlike most animals that I have ever seen, they had great civic sense. You wouldn't ever find their potty littered around your house. In fact for that matter - you would rarely ever see a Cat - crapping. They generally chose a time when no one else was around - and having done their job quietly in some far corner of the garden; they quickly covered up their dispatch with mud. I wish scientists could identify the specific gene responsible for this; and inject it into the multitude of humans who shamelessly relieve themselves astride the railway tracks.

One of the Cats even has a favourite spot where you will always find her sitting in my house – that is, on the ledge of my living-room window. It is a dark corner covered by the overhead tin roof; and if you were in a hurry going-in or coming out of the house, you wouldn't probably notice her sitting there - because she sits so still. I like the way they slowly stretch themselves and flex their bodies. They will arch their backs and turn their tails upward and then holding position for a few moments will gradually relax. When they get an itch on their back - they generally rub themselves on the neem tree in the rear of my house.

I think they come very close in mannerisms to the tiger - the king of the feline species; they can stare back at you with the same intensity and coldness - sending a shiver down your spine. Sometimes they will just not be offended when you try to shoo them away; and will look back at you as if asking, if you really mean it. They are never scared of human presence and walk past you without any hesitation or fear. They have the quiet confidence, that you wouldn't dare disturb them; or even if you tried, they had the means to deal with it. So it was always I who felt the shivers, whenever they crossed too close. They even peed like tigers - that is backwards (raising their tails and facing away from the object on which they wished to shower their blessings).

They also had lately learnt to open the big iron dustbin behind my house; with the heaviest of them (the grandfather I believe) holding down the pedal with his weight, as the others got-in and pulled out whatever drew their interest. In winters they often snoozed in the sun. You could see them sitting quietly and dozing away (with their eyes tightly shut) in some sunny corner of the garden. Or, they would find a spot where the earth having been sufficiently warmed by the sun, was soft and powder-like. And this is where they would roll and park themselves for varying lengths of time.

When it comes to their eating habits - I guess they are omnivorous. However they are great stalkers and prefer to hunt on most days. They can crouch behind a low bush and wait motionless for surprisingly long durations. Or can climb trees and hide themselves up there; to pounce upon a squirrel, a pigeon, or any unsuspecting prey. Having watched them at close, I wonder how people keep Cats as pets. Do they look after them out of love, or is it out of fear? They never seem bound to you by affection; but rather by the need to be fed on time. In fact, given the shrewd and un-trusting temperament of Cats, I am even wary of the people who keep them as pets. Given a choice, I will stand by my German shepherd a thousand times over.

The Parrots

They are really a delight to the eye as they shoot across the sky above. Youth, colorfulness and gay abandon ride on their wings. It is not for nothing that they come forth as arrows from the Cupid's bow. Their deep green plumage, with the black ring at their throats and bright red beaks - are really enticing and allure the observer. They easily hide amongst the trees and are difficult to spot, if they don't move. Their playful whistling and cheeping calls liven up the garden on every occasion. And the sight of Parrots, especially during the monsoons, moves the heart and soul like nothing else can - and easily resuscitates an insipid or a comatose being. An eagerness to live and a host of impossible desires are born in the heart each time one watches the Parrots play in the trees. They love to nibble on the tender guavas, juicy *ber*[30] and the ripe tamarind. In fact if you ever happened to taste a fruit which had been nibbled upon by a Parrot - you would find it most exceptionally sweet. As children we were given to understand (through poems and stories) that Parrots only ate green chilies. But having grown up (an awfully great deal) since then, I have never ever seen a Parrot do just that; even though there was plenty of green chilly growing in my garden.

Parrots are one amongst the most bouncy and flirt full birds that I have seen in my garden. They spend a lot of time necking and edging each other. They while in frolic can even swing around all the way down and then rotate back over the branch or the cable or the vine - on whichever they are perched. They are sporting enough to often hang upside down by their feet or suspend themselves

---

[30] A wild Indian berry

by their beak - before letting go and flying off. Their beaks in particular are razor sharp and can snap awfully hard (as told with conviction by a colleague who once tried to force feed a green chilly to a caged young Parrot).

They nest in the hollow of tree trunks and believe-you-me, it is one of the most beautiful things to see - if you ever could spot a young baby Parrot emerge from his hollow in the early morning sun. I also ardently admire the speed and swiftness with which they fly about and shoot between the trees. I once saw a Parrot so spotless and bright in his colours - that I wondered if he had just been painted upon by an artist. Pet Parrots in India are traditionally nick named- as '*mitthoo*' and are believed to be able to repeat whatever their master's say (of course at a time of their own choosing). So choose your words carefully, if you own a 'mitthoo'.

So much for Parrots; whom I absolutely relish and wish them to be forever in my garden.

Up in the Trees

The Langurs (biological name – *Semnopithecus Entellus*) remind me of another interesting incident (as promised to be recollected in the previous note on Langurs) which came to occur during my days spent in Kasauli (Himachal Pradesh) in the late 80's. Kasauli is a small and beautiful, less discovered and less misshapen hill town, which lies on the way from Chandigarh to Shimla. It has a most mystifying combination of valleys and hillocks, groves and gardens, the urban and the rural and the expected and the unexpected. Just behind where our office was, was a forgotten and undiscovered patch of a deodar forest; and since no one noticed very much (and the urge to cut down trees was not yet fully born) the forest had slowly and silently crept up the slope.

Thus over the years, the gap between our office building and the edge of the forest had closed in. And now it was an easy luxury to be sitting in our office, as well as breathing the invigorating air of the woods at the same time. However, along with the forest came the natives - the Monkeys (biological name – *Rhesus Macaque*). If by chance you left the office window open, they would have quickly glanced through your files and either torn or shredded (believe-me they could use the paper shredder too) or carried-away the most important and urgent of your letters. They had all the freedom to check out your tiffin, raid your pantry, jump on the tin roof, copulate on your windowsills, shake the pipes and the lightening conductors; and thus lay equal claim on this pretty patch of Kasauli. It was the Monkeys who had always been known to be here and never had anyone sited Langurs in this area. They said (that is as the locals told us) that the two never stayed together (or got along well); so it was either the monkeys, or the langurs. But never both in the same place together. And Kasauli, from the time as could be recollected, was a reserve of the monkeys. Langurs generally stayed in the higher and colder reaches and were never seen (as told by the locals again) south of Solan (another hill town ahead of Kasauli, on the way to Shimla). So, the reign of the Monkeys continued in Kasauli.

One morning however, the atmosphere was strange outside; you could smell the tension in the air. The monkey chatter was not to be heard at all. There was an eerie silence. And just as we wondered as to where all the monkeys had gone, we saw them all up the highest of the trees - sitting huddled together; as if in a serious predicament. And then to our utter surprise, what we had never witnessed before was now in front of our eyes - a sizeable bunch of Langurs (comprising the young, old, infants, adolescents and all) were perched on the trees - just opposite to where the monkeys sat. They sat silently and were well aware of the sensitivity of their geographical location. In between both legions, lay the car park (supposedly a no-man's-land). This uneasy calm continued till afternoon; with the monkeys waiting for the langurs to continue their journey (where ever from they had arrived) and to move on (to where ever they were supposed to be going). We waited too, in our offices, aware of the uneasy calm outside.

By noon however, the Langurs hadn't shown any signs of moving on or any indication of their likely intent of doing so. Now the patience of the Monkeys was wearing off and their warning calls and threats to the Langurs were getting sharper and more forthright (clearly audible above the collective noise of our typewriters, Xerox machines and printers). As we peered out of the windows - we saw the Monkeys crossing the car park and making their way (in assault formation) towards the patch where the Langurs had harbored. Soon the langurs were surrounded on all sides and were outnumbered - three is to one. The monkeys began their final charge, marked by the violent shaking of the branches, baring of their teeth and emitting blood-curdling cries. The Langurs got prepared too - not to leave, but to take the challenge head on (adopting a crescent-like defensive formation). And then like all great battles ever fought; this one too resulted in bloodshed, wounds and the abominable war crimes.

However, the skirmish was not in the public eye; both armies mutually consenting to fight it out elsewhere. So, no one knew the outcome – as to who the victor or the vanquished was? God knows to which edge of the forest the warriors had retreated? But then they stayed there for the next five days - perhaps a peace was being brokered? (so we wondered) Or, was there a tactical pause, as fresh reinforcements arrived? One couldn't say. The peace and the quiet now disturbed us more than ever. We grew miserable in this interlude. Our concentration wasn't just the same as before and office work suffered. This period of suspense was to be followed by a weekend. And on Monday we returned to our offices with the same old trepidation. But this time to be greeted, as before, by the good old hoots and monkeys calls. So, the cloud had finally lifted; and we knew who the victors were - of course, our old and familiar monkey brigade. Life was back on track and to our surprise – we happily began sharing larger portions of our tiffins with the monkeys.

But then the next day (that is on Tuesday) the Monkeys were nowhere to be seen (or heard). And believe-you-me, in their place were the dark and large bodied Langurs. And slowly - day by day, the following pattern emerged:

Monday, Wednesday and Fridays	–	Monkeys
Tuesday, Thursday and Saturdays	–	Langurs
And, Sundays	–	Neither of them

The same pattern, without any mix-up (whatsoever), replayed itself for the next three months (and ever thereafter). Until it was clear to us (as daylight) that we were now bequeathed, with the unique distinction of having to serve two masters. It was an unimagined and unparalleled turn of precedence in the quiet history of Kasauli. Who the real victors of the epic battle finally were, was also now evident to the entire staff. The Monkeys, thus, had been unceremoniously routed out (partially so-to-say) from their centuries old home turf. It only heightened our curiosity, as to what must have prevailed during the long face-off, to force such a large humble pie down the narrow throats of our exuberant monkeys. Luckily for us, our gardener's apprentice's wife, who incidentally was out into the forest to pick firewood that day (that is, on the day of the battle), happened to be a reliable witness of the course of events. She, a God fearing and pious woman, never known to have lied in her life - narrated to us (frame by frame) of how the Langurs had overpowered the Monkeys that day.

She told us that the Monkeys having been badly badgered in combat were overpowered one-by-one (by the Langurs) - then tied to the trees and whipped on their backsides (uninterrupted) for three full days. While on the other hand, their women were being unceremoniously molested and their modesty (repeatedly) outraged, by the uncouth langurs. This on the fourth day, broke the collective will of the monkeys (both men and women); and a reluctant peace was thus brokered. Unbelievable though it may seem (to your most honored judgment), but even till today (three decades later) – the old war treaty remains as inviolable and undiluted as ever; with the langurs maintaining their equal grip on monkey land.

All this reinforces the old maxim that 'the scars of a battle sometimes run deep and for generations to come!'

The Way to Panjagutta

Today was the day he would commit suicide. It was decided and final. Rohan didn't find this to be either sensational or a hurried decision. He had it long coming. The whys and why not's were far too many and getting into the past again would only be a waste of time at this juncture.

It seemed like a perfect day. He had returned from college at around three in the afternoon (as usual). Had had his meal of rice, lentils, sautéed vegetables and a bowl of curd; followed by his daily siesta and was up again at around 4.30 pm. Switching on his favorite tape of *Carnatic* music he had slowly and pensively brewed his coffee this evening. One of the things which had made him live his life so far (till today) was undoubtedly Carnatic music. As a small boy, he had learnt it early on for two years and then later (as he grew) while he had given up vocal practice - the love of listening to it daily remained. With coffee not only the music sounded better but the coffee tasted better too.

Having finished coffee, he dressed up carefully and well for the important day that today was. He wanted to be found (when later discovered and reported) - appearing very much the smart and well groomed young man he was. He picked up his mobile, put on his wrist watch and tucked his voter identity in his wallet (he preferred to be later identified and his body to reach his parents). He then locked the door of his paying guest accommodation and descended the stairs; to come out into the side alley of the building shaded by a large *Peepal tree*[31]. As he walked out of the complex the security guard nodded with a smile. Even though it was his last day and last evening so to say - Rohan was not in any kind of hurry. He found himself looking around at the usual sites more keenly than on other days. But then wasn't it natural, when you were passing by or seeing something for the last time - to be inclined to observe it much more closely ?

Rohan was now in the locality of Serilingampally - that is where his paying guest accommodation was in Hyderabad. The plan was not to do it in Serilingampally, but to go to Panjagutta and commit the incident there. As per what Rohan had gathered and come to confirm was that Panjagutta had quite a few unmanned rail-road crossings and a deserted broad-gauge line passing through as well - which was the route for several express and super-fast trains. Today was Friday and there were three trains which Rohan had identified as amongst the preferred ones to mow him down. Of these were a *Shatabdi*[32], a Super-Fast Holiday Special and a *Duronto*[33]. Since all were express racks; any of them would run over him in just no time. He

---

[31] Ficus religiosa or sacred fig; also known as the Bodhi-tree

[32] Series of superfast passenger trains (in India) connecting metro cities

[33] Meaning 'restless' in Bengali language; long-distance nonstop trains (in India)

had mentally played the scene several times over in his mind. It was all very simple - the only thing required of him to do was to be initially standing un-noticed somewhere in close proximity of the railway track (preferably in cover so that no one could accost him or pull him aside at the last moment). Next, Rohan needed to notice the train rushing towards him and then take two small steps and bring himself into the middle of the railway track. Wherefrom it would just be a fraction of a second - when he would be hit by the big engine and it would all be over. There would be no time to feel the pain or to speculate on any irrelevant issues. The hard-hitting initial impact alone would be enough to kill him and his subsequent falling over the track and being minced down by the speeding train would be of no consequence to his consciousness. He had planned to kneel down between the railway lines so that he would be placed squarely and well in the line of the locomotive - and faced no threat of being inaccurately hit or thrown off the railway track.

As per what he had read and studied, train accident victims - almost all of them died instantly and their bodies were generally severed into two or more pieces. But then these were rapid deaths with negligible suffering (as well as survival rates). His identification of course would only be much later; based on his voter identity and the contacts in his mobile phone. And still later, to be delivered to his parents and the rest of the motions settled as are always done in the old and well established ways.

Just outside the gate of the society, about three hundred yards to the East was a *chai-shop*[34]; it was here that he would always hang-out whenever he felt overwhelmed

---

[34] Tea (in Hindi) shop

by the speed or the hollowness of his life. Today for the last time, he felt like a smoke and his favorite *cutting-chai*[35] at this old haunt. He strolled up to the shop and as soon as the shopkeeper saw him, he nodded with familiarity and handed him over (without his asking) a pack of his preferred *'Wills Navy Cut*[36]*'* cigarettes and a match box. Rohan took up the empty cane stool next to the wall and lit-up. Soon the young boy - the shopkeeper's assistant handed him his regular cutting chai. The chai and the cigarettes felt the best today from what they had ever felt before. As the shopkeeper maintained his dues in a small note book and was beginning to note down today's expense in his pad; Rohan waived him over and settled his final account. The shopkeeper asked him if he was leaving Hyderabad, at which Rohan smiled and said "Just shifting".

It was now dark and the street lights, the neon sign boards and the speeding traffic were all in full fury. From Serilingampally (where he was) the travelling time to Panjagutta (by the roadways bus) was about thirty minutes. Further from the Panjagutta bus station it was about fifteen minutes to the broad gauge railway line (by an auto rickshaw). So even if he started right away, he would be in Panjagutta within about forty five minutes; say an hour at the most to be on the safer side. With the time being around 08:30 pm now, he didn't want to be much too early at the railway tracks. The Duronto was expected to pass through Panjagutta only at 10:45 pm and from the current status that he had checked on his mobile - the train was running on time. The other two

---

35 Refers to 'chai' being 'cut' into smaller portions and served in half-glasses

36 A popular brand of Indian cigarettes

trains being both before the Duronto (and people from the slums likely to be walking around at that time) - he had mentally ruled them out. He would take the last one he decided i.e. the Duronto (when the railway tracks would be totally deserted). So, in the intervening time that he had, he decided to sit and wait at the bus stand itself - and in this while make a few calls to his friends (so called) just to chat away and bide his time. He tried to speak to about three of them before he lost interest and gave up the exercise. The first one was driving to somewhere and caught up in traffic when he answered the call (and could barely hear Rohan in the noise). The second one was in a theatre watching a movie. The third was working on a project which he had to submit to the college the next day. And then he had three incoming calls too - the first was from a friend who wanted Rohan to accompany him to a tattoo artist tomorrow - this guy wanted his girlfriend's name tattooed over his back. It quite almost sickened Rohan to see the majority of his friends mushing, pestering and hanging behind their girlfriends most of the time. After all what was in a girl wondered Rohan; to have made dreaming and contemplative baboons of most of his once adventurous colleagues? This business of love was entirely abhorred by him and kept at a good arm's length away. In fact now it suddenly came to him as to how a girl in the second year of his engineering had once tried to hit on him. She had made it a point to bump into him every day in the college canteen and in the painting classes. By and by it had driven Rohan to a state of heightened paranoia and had instilled a morbid fear of the girl in him. And he also remembered how for the balance of the term he had avoided the college canteen and had changed over his activity from painting to clay modeling. It had finally put the girl off-scent and he had felt safe once more.

And then his mother called up too. Reminding him to call-up his father's elder brother who had just got his cataract removed and to enquire about his health. And to call-up his aunt as well - who was soon proceeding with her family on a short vacation to the United Kingdom. All required as part of good etiquette his mother said and to maintain the desired cordiality with one's close relatives. Rohan as usual had no interest in any of this shit. And then the last call was from one of his batch mates - who wanted to borrow his notes as always. Thereafter he had put the phone into the silent mode and slipped it back into his pocket. The time now was getting close and slowly advancing towards the destined hour of his final exit. Rohan got up, stretched his legs and looked around the bus station. Being lost in his thoughts and the telephone calls - quite some time had passed and the bus station had grown a little deserted - not too many people commute too late you know? And even the frequency of the buses reduces a little in the night. Rohan glanced at his watch - 9:00 pm it said; a respectable time for him to get up and get moving to Panjagutta. No, he wasn't rushed or anything - but just that there wasn't much to be done at the bus station and moving on would allow him a change of atmosphere and bring him closer to his objective.

A little hunger pang reminded him that he was still alive. But not being in a mood to eat anything he just bought a bottle of water and drowned the craving in his stomach. Then looking out at the information board, he waited for Bus Number 349 - to cover yet another leg of his journey. Despite having waited for about twenty minutes, Bus number 349 was nowhere to be seen. It was now getting tight. He had no further time to while away. To lead to the desired fulfillment of his plan the next phase of his journey ought to commence right away. Or else he would be exposing himself to the risk of missing his appointment. The clarity of purpose and his firm resolve spurred Rohan to explore other alternatives.

Perhaps he should ask someone who was a regular on this route and so Rohan looked around. Only a few people were to be seen. At the far end of the bus station a flower woman sat with her basket on the floor - counting out her day's earnings in coins. A man with a sack of onions was standing a few paces away - smoking his *bidi*[37]; and two old temple priests in white *dhotis*[38] and with sandal wood paste on their foreheads sat talking a few benches ahead of him. Rohan first approached the priests who were the closest – and politely asked them the connection to Panjagutta. Looking at him disdainfully (for no apparent reason), one of them brusquely said "Don't know! Ask someone else." Next, the man with the onions - was a rustic villager. He spoke only in vernacular (his village dialect) which Rohan didn't understand. Now remained the old flower woman - who too seemed unlikely to know the way to Panjagutta, but Rohan had no option left but to ask her as well. So he moved towards her end of the bus station. Just then a bus rolled-in and he saw a young woman get down quickly. She seemed suave and educated and Rohan hopefully moved towards her to make his query. When he approached she was looking the other way and he politely

---

[37] A type of cheap cigarette made of unprocessed tobacco wrapped in Tendu (*Diospyros melanoxylon*) leaves

[38] Also known as vetti or mundu is a traditional men's garment worn in the Indian subcontinent

said – "Excuse me, by any chance would you know how to get to Panjagutta? The 349 doesn't seem to be coming along". And then, as the young lady turned to look towards him, saying "Panjagutta?" - their eyes met; and suddenly it seemed as if large clouds of flowers had burst somewhere high above in the sky and that rose petals were falling all over. Her voice was magical, as if an angel played the sweetest lute there ever was in heaven. Rohan's voice barely came through but still he managed to say "Yes, Panjgutta!" And then he noticed her eyes - like large lakes; those with crystal waters which lie undiscovered in the mountains. Her face was the radiance of a thousand moons drawn together - a seemingly impossible dream. The complexion was a matted gold and her braided hair fell far below her waist, like a thick tassel of silk. She had fresh *mogra*[39] knitted in her hair - and he could smell their sweetness. Her lips were like the petals of a flower which he never had seen in his life. Just as he felt self-conscious for gawking; she told him that the 349 had lately been discontinued. But of course there was another connection and that she was going to Panjagutta too. And he could come along. Within minutes a bus arrived which they swiftly boarded. And as providence would have it, less for two empty seats together all others were taken.

Taking the aisle seat Rohan allowed the lady to be seated next to the window. And as the bus moved on he had only one prayer on his lips – that of his arriving well within time at his rendezvous. The lady remarkably bold, confident and completely unaware of how her presence tormented his senses; asked him where he studied? And then she told him that her college was in Serilingampally

[39] Or the Arabian jasmine is a sweetly fragrant white flower

too (very close to where Rohan stayed). And that she was in the final year of her Software Designing. Rohan meanwhile had unwittingly drifted away like an honest skiff on a powerful current (simply studying the flow of water around him). She was the prettiest of the girls that he had ever set eyes upon in his long and insipid life. While she was tender and delicate in her semblance - her self-assurance set her aflame. He noticed the *'alta*[40]' decoration of a classical dancer on her dainty feet; and then also the litheness and the poetic grace in her movements. And her eyes, deeply expressive, brimmed with a natural liveliness.

Rohan pulled himself apart from the flow of the current and looked at his watch. He still had sufficient time to make it. Well she said she was Niharika (one to be looked at admiringly - and how apt he thought) and then the introductions followed. Next, taking out an entry pass to a College Fest she handed it over to Rohan - asking him to come over and see her dance performance the next day at her college (if he had the time that is). "And wouldn't he come?" She asked. Rohan felt a strange trepidation tug at his heart and found that he had answered with "Yes, of course I'll be there. My college is only next door" (he didn't have the heart to lie to her and dampen her spirits). "Oh! What fun that would be" said Niharika and "I'll show you my college too after the performance. And then we can enjoy our Canteen's special *masala dosa*[41] and cold coffee as well!" Rohan by now was trying to fathom the swirl of strange emotions which rose within his chest. Meanwhile

40 Or Mahawar or Rose Bengal is a red dye which women in India apply with cotton on the border of their feet

41 A fermented crepe made from rice batter and stuffed with lightly cooked potatoes(a staple dish in South India)

she had opened up her tiffin and had brought about Rohan to be happily sharing the same with her. Unguarded over the sandwiches, Rohan caught himself sharing his fondness for Carnatic music with Niharika. Surprisingly to be echoed back that it was her fervent passion too and how along with classical dance it fed her life and soul. She seemed to have opened up so much so fast with Rohan that to him it felt as if they were old friends; or that there existed a long shared connection between them. Strange! Or how weird! Or whatever thought Rohan to himself (Niharika surprisingly was thinking the same too). But secretly (despite his immediate plans) - somewhere deep down (unknown even to himself) he wished this journey together to be an unending one. He however was still happy that this brief sequence had somehow fitted-in before the final fall of the curtains of his play. And then drawing his mind back to the impending mission, he heard Niharika exclaim – "Here comes Panjagutta! Let's get down quick! And Rohan can you take my bag please?" (And immediately wondering as to what was in this boy to make her so very comfortable with him?)

Standing at Panjagutta Bus Station as she straightened up her dress, it was now time for each to go his own way - Niharika on her long journey ahead and Rohan to a swift culmination of his brief voyage. As Rohan looked at his watch – it said 10:00 pm. With only forty five minutes left for the Duronto to pass over, Rohan was already looking around for any waiting auto rickshaws - because from here it was about twenty minutes to the broad-gauge railway line. Niharika took her bag from Rohan and slung it across her shoulder. And then shyly (or rather a bit self-consciously) mentioned the need for him to take her telephone number - just so that it would be easy to contact her when he came to the College Fest the next day. "Of course" said Rohan. And so the telephone numbers too were exchanged.

Niharika suddenly said "Hope you are feeling fine? You seemed to have been pre-occupied all the while that we travelled and look a little pale even now". "No! I am perfectly fine" said Rohan and "May be the heat is just making me a little faint, nothing more."

"Well! Which way are you going Rohan?" asked Niharika. "Oh! Ya towards the Panjagutta railway siding - where the broad-gauge rail line passes through" blurted Rohan; and then immediately regretting not having come up with a better answer. "I'll just wait for an auto" he added.

"But then don't you know that autos don't ply after 10 pm in Panjagutta? And in any case, where would you go from near the railway tracks? That area is really one deserted end of the town!" remarked Niharika.

"To my aunt's house close by" shot back Rohan.

"Are you sure?" said Niharika. "But then there's no colony or houses there as far as I remember" she added. Rohan bent over and pretended to tie his shoe lace - he didn't want his face to give away any sign of discomposure (if at all there was). However, a sudden anxiety and nervousness had already descended over him - for he wondered how he would be getting to his chosen location without any autos running at this hour. His palms were wet with sweat. But Niharika's question still needed an answer - and keeping a straight face he replied "But she's only recently moved in and you perhaps wouldn't have noticed the recent developments in that area". Niharika shrugged her shoulders. And then she made an offer that Rohan couldn't refuse. It seemed the only way possible that he could (if ever) make it to his rendezvous in time today.

Niharika since she stayed in Panjagutta, would every morning come on her scooter to the Bus station; park her scooter in the parking lot and then catch a bus to where ever she was supposed to be going. In the evening on reaching back she would once more take her scooter and drive back home. Tonight even though she was unusually late because of her dance rehearsal, she still offered (for some unexplained reason) to drop Rohan at his destination before heading home. Rohan jumped at the suggestion. It was his last remaining chance.

Niharika was a confident and bold driver. And he even though on the pillion was careful to maintain a proper physical distance from Niharika. He had never known a girl to be so exceedingly attractive and confident and someone sharing the same interests too. And of course so spontaneous in her association, in such short a time. Niharika on the other hand wondered why in her entire college and all her years of studying - she had never ever come across as quiet, self - possessed, sober and nice a boy as Rohan. She had kind of felt something the very first moment they had spoken at Serilingampally (though she couldn't say what it exactly was). And even while she had led the conversation all through; Rohan had participated with a visible keenness and had made no move or statement to make her in any way feel uncomfortable. There was something about him which made her want to see him tomorrow at her college fest and again and again and again. But then saying so would seem rather premature and make her appear crass - and so it was all quiet; as normal decorum warranted.

It was dark and deserted as she turned her scooter towards the railway siding. Not a soul was to be seen. Even though staying in Panjagutta for years, she had known well to keep away from this desolate end of the town. They reached a crossroads and she asked Rohan "Which way is your aunt's house?" This seemed to have stumped him and he said "You just drop me anywhere close to the broad-gauge rail line and I'll make my way thereafter. And thanks for being such a great help".

Well if she had her way she would have liked to spend some more time with Rohan on the pillion and drop him all the way to his aunt's house; but then fine, she would just drop him off at the rail line as he wanted, thought Niharika. Reaching the broad-gauge rail line she brought the scooter to a halt. She was going to miss him; but then he was going to be with her at the college fest tomorrow - and such and similar thoughts raced through her mind.

Why had Niharika not arrived earlier in his life? Why had it to be only today? And why had it to be only her - dropping him off at his final destination? What was this strange attraction that he felt for a girl whom he had barely spent an hour with? Where had she been all these years? But all these were pointless musings (though they very much did flit across his mind as he dismounted). Mustering up a warm smile he genuinely appreciated Niharika's help and told her how so very much he had enjoyed her company. Then thanking her he turned and walked off - like a man with a purpose.

Niharika wondered if he was fine. Even though he had smiled and spoken well, he appeared to be in a kind of a stupor and cut off from the whole scene. As if pre-occupied with some bigger concerns of his own. She turned to look back at him. In the darkness she saw his shrinking form already quite a distance away; and slowly growing even smaller. Suddenly it seemed as if she heard an old tune sailing on the warm summer breeze - but then she was tired after a long day.

Rohan caught himself singing an old song, which he was surprised he had even known or remembered so well. He felt light, almost liberated - even though there was a new and sweet sadness in his heart. He was happy and looked forward to soar in the skies and being amidst the constellations high above (even as he felt he was leaving behind some unfinished story). Now he was running between the railway lines - and had over taken all his life's miseries and unfairness. All alone he was. With the wind sweeping his face; he unbuttoned his shirt as he ran and threw if off. Running bare chested he was crying with ecstasy. And a thrill - unfamiliar so far, was shaking his body from within. Running towards it - he saw a light approaching to meet him on the railway line - and then the long shrill horn of the Duronto pierced his ears. Then the light grew sharper and closer - speeding towards him - swiftly approaching - and then the horn again and the heavy and powerful crunching sound of the engine - which was now overwhelming. And then the time of his running was over. Spent and awash with tears; mind numb and body shaking (with an ecstatic sobbing) - he knelt down between the rail lines. And as planned (and played out so many times in his mind) he now faced the Duronto - almost upon him with its deafening roar. The ground below him shook with the increasing proximity of the gargantuan force. With the glare of the Duronto blinding his vision, the heat of the locomotive was now upon him; and he - just a nano second away for everything to be over forever. And then there was a crash, and a powerful jolt threw him aside - as the Duronto brushed past his skin. He lay on the gravel astride the track - his face pressed down to the ground and held there by a strong panting body.

Rohan shook uncontrollably - his crying mixed with the passing sound of the Duronto. Tears flowing, he felt he was dead; but then the weight which had pinned him down made him aware that he still breathed. The force which held him only increased with the rushing past of the Duronto. And as the last coach went by - it set him free. With his body numb, he slowly rolled over on his back. And as he peered into the darkness, he saw a weeping moon bent over his face. The warm and incessant tears of which fell on him and seemed to wash him anew. Then the voice of Niharika came through, shaking him hard and repeatedly asking only one question – "Why Rohan? Why? What was the need? What was the need for you to be ending it all? Was it so bad?"

Rohan felt he had died under the Duronto that day, and was now being born again. The tight knot of anguish and pain deep within him had been undone and seemed to have dissolved away. The misery of the world too, appeared to have gone past with the speeding train. Now things were different. He was not alone anymore. His old loneliness was a thing of the past. Together, they walked back slowly - hand-in-hand - now and forever. He needed no one anymore thereafter. And the bitterness could never reach him again. That night Niharika took him home and introduced him to her parents. They asked her no questions; like they had always never asked her. Only trusting, trusting and trusting.

Niharika's dance performance at the college fest the next day was fired with a new zeal and was a stupendous hit; with Rohan watching and applauding from the front row. Then they ambled together holding hands; soaking in the crazy atmosphere of the college fest and the intensity of their new found togetherness. The coffee and the dosa which they shared in the college canteen that day - seemed to both to be the best meal they had ever eaten. And Rohan slowly came to believe - how not everything is hollow and how not everything is blown away by the wind; and how the sands of time however persisting cannot erode away some quintessential bonds.

After the college fest, as they stepped out on the road and were moving towards the parking lot - a passing cab suddenly braked to a halt. And as they approached, the driver rolled down his window and asked "Can you please tell me the way to Panjagutta?" And then, he forever was left to wonder – 'As to why that day - the boy and the girl had so surreptitiously smiled to each other before giving him the directions to Panjagutta?'

Butterflies

(Today he was a grown up man (into his late forties to be exact). And as he sat in the garden this evening, sipping his tea and looking at the young nasturtiums and hollyhocks, old memories blossomed and he shared one such thought (more of a self-confession) with his little boy)

'I have seen some of the most amazing and colourful butterflies as a kid, when we stayed for a short while in Arunachal. But it was only much later that I understood their true worth.

I learnt from friends that the average life span of a butterfly is just about eight to ten days; and when I heard that, a grave sense of guilt came over me as I recollected all those butterflies that I had caught as a kid and pressed so mercilessly between the pages of my Phantom and Mandrake comics.

If God gave them so little time to live, I wonder why he put such beautiful colours and exquisite designs on their wings. Why didn't he simply make all the butterflies black?

And if they have such short life spans, why don't the butterflies just sit down quietly under a bush and brood, waiting gloomily for their fast approaching death?

Instead, I find them flying with gay abandon, hopping from flower to flower and some of them I have even seen flying real high in total violation of their expected low flying traditions (imagine violating traditions and even breaking thresholds, in just a life of about ten days!). In their short life spans, they even fall in love; I say so because I've seen them mating.

I think they are teaching us a lesson or two by the way they live their lives.

It is not the span of our lives that matters but how much colour and beauty we epitomize and how much fun and meaning we pack into our days which really count.

Just look at ourselves; do we know the span of our lives? What if it is only ten days! So why don't we live a little more like butterflies? While we see some of the butterflies flying around today, let us learn a lesson as we acknowledge their spirit and salute their attitude towards life.'

A Plea

(From the recollections of a man who had a habit of walking alone in the gardens)

'It was a rather short apple tree, heavily laden with large red apples; but what caught my eye were not the apples but a dove lying under the tree. The dove was one of those common brown ones you generally see sitting on telephone lines. It was now dead.

The sight made me feel sad. Within my chest I felt as if I was in some way responsible for the death of this dove; let us call him John. As a kid whenever I saw beautiful birds in the sky I would wonder – do they ever die? If they do, why don't I ever see any dead birds which have just dropped out of the sky? And today in the death of John, I felt as if my old childhood curiosity was being answered. I felt therefore a deep sense of guilt for having ever wondered such things as a kid.

I bent down and gently picked up John from the ground. It was the first time I had ever held a dove. From the look and feel of it, it was rather clear that John had died not too long back. His body was still warm and supple, his feathers soft and clean. I searched for any visible signs of injury on John's body but couldn't find a scratch. From the appearance John looked perfectly healthy, but now he was dead.

I wondered how he had died. Where was his family as he was dying? And do his wife and kids know that he is now lying here, dead, under this apple tree? Or do they innocently await him in their nest; his wife looking forward to sharing the happenings of the day with him and his children planning some games with their dad? Did John die all of a sudden? Or had he succumbed to a long illness? So many questions were running through my mind.

What all had John accomplished in his life? Did he have some things which he treasured? Was he close to his family? Did he love his wife and kids fiercely? Hope he was not from an indifferent family, where no one really understood him. Although I never knew John, but now holding him in my hands I felt strangely connected to him. What a sad way for two strangers to meet for the first time.

I wish and would like to believe that John had lived a happy and wholesome life. Now as I held his lifeless body in my hands, I wondered whether I had ever seen John while he was alive; was he ever one amongst the so many several doves I had seen in the sky? He had a sense of peace and calm from his appearance. All his trivial struggles in life had now ended. All his links to whatever he had achieved, held close to his heart or built or cherished in his life had now been severed. He seemed as ordinary as any of those birds in the sky which we don't really have time to notice. They are hardly in a position to commit any great sin in their life; then why this death in total loneliness? and now surrounded by unknown, uncaring and indifferent people.

Though out of habit (since men are not expected to cry) my eyes remained dry, but my heart shed a tear for John. I hope no one; no one at all in this world ever gets a death like John. It is inevitable that we all must die one day. But to be all alone in one's final moments, in some unknown orchard, under an unknown apple tree and later to be picked up by unknown people – it just doesn't seem fair at all.

Please God - don't do to us what you did to John.'

Seasons

(No, he wasn't from the metrological department and neither was he a student of geography; but then his understanding of the climate and seasons was unique. He believed that)

'God made the seasons so that we may understand the mysteries of life.

The trees that stand so tall and proud today, loaded with green leaves, are the very same ones which had lost all their leaves in autumn and once stood naked in the sun, solemn but yet not losing their patience. The barren and bare mountains remain covered under heavy snow for eight to ten months each year, yet they do not perish and it is their perseverance which makes us witness the most beautiful flora which blossoms amidst the rocks once the snow melts.

In monsoons, the rains come and the skies remain dark and pouring water relentlessly for days together. The whole world seems wet and gloomy, yet in the end the sun comes out and our world is once again full of sunshine and warmth. You can see the birds fluff and dry their feathers and hop around in boundless joy.

In summers, the heat burns the earth and every living creature faces the fury of the sun. It seems everything will wither away and perish; but then one day, most unexpectedly and out of nowhere an army of black clouds appear in the skies. They simply block out the sun. You soon begin to feel a new coolness in the air and the environment becomes still and silent – as if waiting for something; and then - pearls of pure water begin their rush down from the skies and the whole earth with all its withered life is washed up in the cool showers and is once again rejuvenated. Just like before, the world seems happy and young.

It's quite so with our lives; sometimes everything seems gloomy and there appears to be no reason to live, but then when it is time, God changes the seasons of our life.

Sometimes we keep on failing and life becomes a string of defeats with nothing going right. We must understand that this is the summer of our lives, and should endeavor to preserve the seeds of patience and hope within us. Soon (which may however seem like an eternity), when the time is ripe, God brings in the monsoons. Success suddenly pours down from the skies and there are pools of joy all around.

At times we have to struggle and life seems really hard; that is the time to keep our chin up and continue the struggle. No matter how dark the nights of our life, it is certain that the full moon shall rise, shooting down all the dark shadows and filling up the sky with soft and golden moonshine.

Just like winter, autumn, summer and spring; sadness, sorrow, joy and thrill are some of the seasons of our life. Though life is full of victories and defeats; failures never last forever and success is the time to plan and work for greater heights. So let us live each season of our lives with full courage and cheer. In the winter, let us not forget the sun; and in the summer, let us not forget the rain.'

A House in the Forest

It was a thick forest. After a point the dirt track grew overgrown with shrubs, bushes and creepers - and then it couldn't be made out anymore. We didn't know how to go in any further. Squeezing oneself through the high bushes seemed the only way. Within minutes we were in the thick of it; and whichever way we looked, it seemed as good as North. Just then, over the top of the trees we saw an old house trying to get some fresh air. At least somebody lived here and that made us feel better. We turned towards the direction of the house and would have walked about twice of an hour when we came across a wide moat which lay all around it. And since no one seemed to be lowering a bridge for us, we made handy a wooden log and went across. The other side was thick bush too. It looked like no one had been going-in or coming-out a long time. The windows were all shut and we didn't see no door. The plaster peeled in places and the pathways were covered with moss. How old the house really was is difficult to say; since not much sunlight came in through the trees.

There were other houses around there too. But all were built far apart from each other. It seemed every one lived independently and without much interaction. But then let's only talk of the house upon which we chanced to venture. I guess it wasn't as old as it was unmaintained. There stood a pond which was dry and overgrown, branches from the overhead trees lay where they had fallen, heaps of dry leaves crowded the sidewalk and a section of the roof seemed to have been blown off by a storm. Surely not an inviting house you may say. But at the same time not one that you dare not approach. We advanced a little more, till it became obligatory for us to step into thorny and thick undergrowth. And as yet no sign of a door or a living presence was noticeable to the eye.

I admit that this surely scared and discouraged us; for who wants ever to willingly draw trouble upon one's self. But we were a courageous lot and making up our minds we approached the house from the East. Harried and bruised we reached at the cobbled path - but the East face was simply a solid stone wall; less one window which was made so high up from the ground that it couldn't be peeped into (only allowing someone inside to look out). We went to the North face - this too had two windows very high up (even higher than the one on the East face) and covered with heavy blinds. It all seemed really strange to us; but then in a forest it's not uncommon to not be surprised. The South face of the house finally made us heave a sigh of relief. It was just the face you would expect any normal house to have – there stood a grand entrance - a beautiful door with lilies and juniper growing both sides and a row of potted daisies and bright chrysanthemums along the wall. There also was a mail box to the left of the door (though I wondered - if ever a postman made it here). To the right and a little high up was a name plate. And as very much expected of a country house, there was a lion-head brass knocker in the middle of the door.

Encouraged, we walked over. And as I put out my hand to reach the brass knocker on the dark mahogany door - I couldn't believe it – the knocker wasn't really there! My hand simply grabbed thin air. It was kind of just painted there. What a rude prank to play on someone; and that too in the middle of a thick forest. Anyway my knuckles came in handy - and I gave a good rap on the thick door. Ouch! They cracked at the contact - the door wasn't there too – again only painted on the wall (thankfully it hadn't been painted 'wide open' or I might have broken my face). Now looking closely, the picture (quite literally) became clear - it was all a façade – a painted appearance - merely a false front - just to make it all look very familiar and inviting (until you made up your mind and knocked). The lilies, the daisies, the petunias, the chrysanthemums and even the tall bougainvillea - were all the work of an expert artist. Even the bamboo plant and the juniper on the sides - was a hoax. But hey! The mail box was real. Only that it was open from below and right under it was a small trash bin; so if somebody dropped-in a letter - it would fall out of the bottom and turn straight into garbage. Funny! I thought. We now had to read the guy's name on his nameplate. It couldn't have been more weird - painted in red, over a white board it said 'Trespassers will be prosecuted'. I looked back for reassurance; just in time to see my friends bolting away at top speed – and melting into the forest. So it was now just the two of us - me and myself – all alone at the painted door! I didn't know what to expect next. Unlike my friends, I couldn't bring myself to suddenly break into a run - maybe a Rottweiler waited in the bushes, just to chase me; or may be a guy was out there with a gun to take a shot at a running target? But what really went against my running – honestly - was simply a bad pair of knees. And then it seemed I heard someone coughing from the window high above (wherein I naturally couldn't see). Pressing my back to the wall, I slowly traversed around the corner.

And there at the back - I saw inviolable proof of human existence; there was a row of cabbages and a patch of aborigines - just watered. Surely somebody was living and tending the garden (my friends in their frantic running, I concluded, couldn't have stopped by to water the plants). And as I stepped across the vegetable patch - there right under the birch tree - was a folding table with reading glasses and a chair next to it.

This undoubtedly was intruding into someone's private space; but by now I was way too curious to give a damn. Finally I found it expertly camouflaged behind an overgrown cactus – a narrow door (as a door really should be). I pushed and peeped in through the gap. The light was very dim inside - a small yellow bulb glowed far away at the end of a long corridor. As I stepped in I noticed the corridor was far too narrow. So narrow that not even two people could walk together side by side. Even as I walked alone I was pressed in by the walls on either side. Cold wind blew from the opposite end. I pulled up my collar and kept my step. The corridor was long and winding. Then turning in loops it went on intersecting itself; till finally I couldn't say whether I was walking ahead or simply going in circles. Both sides of the corridor I noticed were lined with doors; doors which were all alike. I was really skeptical as to what lay on the other side. May be all the rooms were locked or empty or simply containing old furniture or something just as harmless; but then if it happened to be something bad - it could even be the worst.

Hesitatingly I placed my hand on one of the doors. And just as I pressed a little with my fingertips to confirm whether the room was locked or otherwise - the door swung open. The light inside was very bright - it seemed the middle of a sunny afternoon. A boy of about ten, wearing knee long denim shorts came cycling towards me at full speed - and then braked just short of the big toe of my right foot. He didn't even look at me or rather seemed not to notice me at all; as if I didn't exist. Getting down from his bicycle the boy came close and picked up a bright blue marble from the ground. He laughed with uninhibited joy. It was a wild and spontaneous laugh that I myself hadn't heard or laughed since I was long a kid. He was trailed by a golden cocker spaniel (it reminded me of Ginger – our old dog). Putting the marble in his pocket the boy speeded away. Things such as kites, a cricket bat, roller skates and stuff like that was littered all around the room. There was also the boy's slam book lying there - on a table next to the television. As I turned the first page - it was the things that the boy wanted to be when he grew up - a trapeze artist at the circus, a train driver, a deep sea diver, a pirate, a painter or Phantom's closest ally. I walked a bit more into the room till I heard some shouting and turned to see the boy and his friends now play cricket. The boy was at the crease and hit the ball really hard - that sent it flying across the room. It in fact missed me closely. Not wanting an injury, I turned back and exit the room.

As I closed the door behind me the corridor was as quiet as before. Not a sound escaped the room. I walked a few paces and tried another door. It opened the same way as the previous one. And inside – there was a small cottage on a hill. The boy was not to be seen playing around anymore. I wondered if he was out with his friends. However on entering the cottage - I found him studying in his small room. Even though he studied intently it was evident that he didn't like it one bit. He had no time left to paint or fly kites or shoot paper planes anymore. The mood in the house was somber - no music, no television, no laughter and no surprises. Everything was in order. Even the cocker spaniel pretended to be asleep on a rug in the corner of the boy's study. I felt a little short of fresh air and came back out of the room.

The next room I walked into – opened onto a railway platform. A young bespectacled man was boarding a train. His luggage was now loaded and his folks were seeing him off. The man had finished his studies and had got his first job. As the train left I wondered where the young playful boy was – until it struck me that the boy had grown up and had just left on the train. I then saw the boy settling into his job with no time to know anything outside his routine. His heart seemed not to be in there with him. But then getting incentives for all his toiling he carried on in the race. Lest my presence disturbs the office work, I left the boy alone with his boss.

The next room was all a mess – diapers sat with books and baby clothes and toys were littered all over. A young woman breezed past, cursing that the milk would have boiled over by now. And our bespectacled boy, now a man; rushing after her like the cocker spaniel of his childhood. Sorry, he said. He was really and extremely sorry for whatever he had said. He hadn't meant a word of it - he assured her. He said it wasn't entirely his fault; he had grown up with used to behaving like this and to respond commonly in such manner - which the young woman was now finding most inconsiderate, selfish and unacceptable. How could our young boy be always only thinking of himself? She wondered. His apologies were sincere - so she just ignored them and carried on with warming the milk for the kids. Our friend now had a family going. I could see the young man put all his interests aside and devote whatever best of his time he could to the family. There was much rushing and far too many things happening at the same time. I could barely find a place to stand without being pushed or collided into. I twice attempted to greet the young man and also to ask him for some directions - but each time he simply rushed past occupied with his mindless racing.

Outside it was all quiet, eerie and cold in the corridor. Since it was getting late, I hurried a little and skipped a few rooms on the way. The next I checked on - had a man sitting on an easy chair with his back to the door. He wore glasses and was reading a book. With thin grey hair - this man was surely past his prime. As he looked up I noticed the sunken cheeks, the bags under the eyes and the detached look on his face. And the man was faintly familiar too. Wait! Wasn't he the young man I had last seen? And then his missus comes in from the adjoining kitchen and rags our man for lazing around all day. She says there's much to be done - walking the dog, cleaning the garage, watering the plants, mopping the toilet floor, ironing the clothes, getting the grocery - and that our man is simply unaware and lost in his own world. The remaining of the couple's conversation was drowned in the combined sounds of the television, the FM radio, the mobile ringing, the microwave beeping, something grinding in the mixer, the washing machine and the cuckoo clock. Our man got up – put on his shoes - picked up a list of things to be done from the dresser and taking his wallet, cap and the car keys advanced towards the door – just next to which I stood huddled. He walked as close to my nose but somehow failed to notice me. I was just about to say hello! When he closed the door in my face and walked out. I rushed after him but he was gone. The corridor was empty as before. It was all too strange. For a while it seemed I was trespassing on someone's entire life. But then forests are known to be confronting one with the unexpected.

I carried on. And now wanting to simply get out of the house I ran along the corridor; which just didn't seem to end. In this I think I skipped the next ten to fifteen rooms. And now as I stood apparently at the end of the corridor – I was tempted to check out at least the last two rooms. One of them had an old man all alone by himself. He lay on his cot - perhaps very ill - and breathing heavily. An assortment of medicines lay all piled up on a chest close by. There was not a soul around and the silence was deep and deafening. And the last room surprisingly was empty. Not even a piece of furniture in there. Our old man was missing too. The room was entirely bare; except for an empty cot standing against the wall and some old photo albums gathering dust in a corner.

I rushed out of the back door. And as I emerged - it was already dark. In the beam of my pocket flashlight I began making my way back. As I passed by the painted face of the house - I observed that some mail had meanwhile gathered in the open dust bin (remember - the one below the mail box). So a postman did visit, I thought to myself. Wanting to at least know the name of the house owner - I quickly picked up an envelope from the trash bin and thrust it into my pocket. Just then an owl hooted from the tree above and I could hear the distant howling of the jackals.

Turning once more to look at the house; I seemed to see strange shadows moving across the windows and I bet I heard a piercing cry. Quickly calculating my chances - I turned my back on the house and shot through the forest like a wild boar.

After venturing over several false trails; which ended abruptly at ponds, a spring, at the edge of a steep cliff and at the mouth of a blind cave - I finally hit the one which brought me out of the forest. Getting back home all bruised and badgered - I crossed myself, washed up and then warmed the half-finished cup of coffee I had left behind by my bedside. Just as I had tucked in - I suddenly remembered the envelope which lay in my coat pocket. I got up and fished it out with a strange trepidation. Then by the light of my bed lamp, carefully putting on my glasses I held up the envelope - to read on it – 'My own name and address!'

Billions of blue blistering barnacles! - As Captain Haddock would say under the circumstances; it certainly was some big mix-up or maybe it was the stale coffee which made my head to reel. How possibly could this be? But then cold wind blew in through the corridor and pulling my blanket over my head, I dozed off.

Good Manners

(A word about good manners, from a man with remarkable natural ability for ice hockey)

'Ice Hockey is a beautiful game, seems effortless. The ice itself is remarkable - exceptionally smooth, and thus making the sliding about so easy. But why am I talking here of ice hockey, when the chosen subject is 'good manners'? Anyway let us continue with ice hockey for a while.

If you have been to Canada or to North America you would have surely watched the game live. Or if like me, you haven't had the chips to travel abroad, you would have surely watched the sport on television. So you would have noticed, how the players slide about; and not to forget the 'puck' (serving the purpose of a 'ball') in the game, how so swiftly and smoothly it glides on the ice. All the 'puck' needs is a small push from the hockey. And if it is a hard-strike (like it sometimes is), how very fast - like a bullet, the puck ricochets off from the walls and corners and keeps going around, till one of the players having had enough, stops it with his or her stick.

Enough of ice hockey (though playing a game is never enough). Let us now move on to the subject major.

Though like a perfect gentleman (generally) one is well mannered and respects women, and is adequately convinced of how rude or improper it is, to measure them up (from bottom to top), or to take stock of their physical assets, or to look at them in a drooling way, or to think other ambitious and outrageous thoughts; but it sometimes so happens - that while one is really innocent, and well-meaning and helpless, somehow some faint trigger (unsuspectingly) releases the hammer - and the game has begun. You are now sliding on ice, really fast and with no support. All of a sudden you have become an unknowing player, in a fast moving game.

Quite often, and to my embarrassment, it has happened that some beautiful women have made an unknowing ice hockey player out of me. Say I started to engage them in a most decent and gentlemanly way. Like say, I was simply talking about the weather, or the movies, or the traffic, or the rising prices etc. - and all of a sudden, there is a devastating distraction. Everything is ruined. Believe me, it was always them who made the first move.

Let me amplify this a bit further. Say it is a beautiful woman to whom you are talking to. And are looking into her eyes while speaking, giving her all the due respect (which is but natural); and of course wanting her to draw the right conclusions about you. But say she happens, unfortunately, to be attractive and on top of that is wearing a low neck T-shirt, or a sleeveless shirt, or perhaps a shirt with deep cuts under the armpits, a short skirt, or may be an extremely tight or a low cut jeans. And just when it is all going very well, like an honorable and harmless conversation; it so happens, that the pen decides to accidently slip out of the woman's well-manicured hands, and she all of a sudden (without warning you) bends to pick it up, and in this – is revealed her cleavage. Or say, the woman just gets up to leave, to fetch something (perhaps a glass of water), affording you a glimpse of her most tight fitting jeans from the rear; or say, the woman just casually raises her arm to flick back a lock of hair from her face, and in that, is accentuated her slender neck or a smooth shaven armpit. And believe me any of this can be utterly devastating.

It is like precious and well preserved chinaware breaking. Sorry, but now it's too late. The ice hockey has begun; with your gaze viz. the 'puck' slipping helplessly back and forth, or to and fro, from her face to her arms, or neck, or waist, or armpits etc. This, while one is still trying (hopelessly) to make sense of the conversation and regain one's balance. But it is all just ruined. The hard work of trying to make an impact, to appear different, to create an honorable impression, is all washed away in no time.

The woman instantly knows (with conviction) how your eyes (and imagination) have wandered and gone astray; and how your shallow mind is now ticking. It is really embarrassing - very very embarrassing. And what makes it even further pathetic, is, as to how one is still trying to appear in control and innocently detached from the game.

But then if you play ice hockey, it is all quite obvious. It just cannot be hidden. Your opponent knows. But then why does it make one feel so miserably guilty? It isn't entirely our fault; we didn't start it in the first place. It was always 'them' who made the first move; always and every time. And we were simply watching (quite literally).

So, beautiful women must know how easy it is for them to have us sliding on ice. And once started how naturally it goes. So, here's a small appeal to all the beautiful women out there (on behalf of all well-meaning men like me) – Please be considerate. Do not without forewarning, undertake any sudden or un-thinking actions, such as flicking back your hair, bending to pick up a pen, crossing your legs, raising your arm to point to the sky or getting up suddenly to leave the room or any such serious movements. Please have mercy, and keep your movements measured and slow. Thank you. Amen.'

Nothing Funny

A donkey is a funny animal. That's what everyone believes. But for myself I really cannot say if it has any sense of humour. So far as I am told, it has always been lifting heavy loads and has never cracked a joke. It however has a hoarse cry which not only didn't make me laugh but rather to wonder, as to how it had come to be. The reason I discovered is that, as its mother gave birth to its first born; the apes in the trees above made so much fun of the poor animal and called it so many names – that its mother cried and cried and cried – till she had lost her voice. Never to get it back again. But then the story doesn't end here. Coming back to the apes, they thought they were the smartest animals around; so much so that they even started walking upright, wearing clothes and brushing their teeth. In their act to be what they were not, they lost a lot of their monkey traits. But along with that they also lost their character and integrity. And of the present I am told – most of them (as they evolved) are mentally sick and have long forgotten who they are. Thus remaining neither chimps nor what they started out to be. Their current stock is now an utterly despicable and a fast mutating (spineless) species. And this I am told is the curse of the donkey.

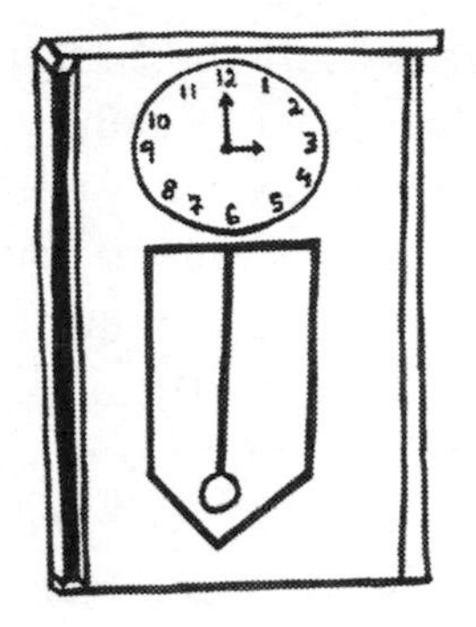

The Ticking of a Clock

Rahim was a repairer of old Clocks. There was no clock on a wall anywhere, that given, he couldn't repair. His family had known time across generations; from his great grandfather's time to the days that now passed. And though acknowledging the universal pervasiveness and unhindered march of time, he had nevertheless devised his own small way of standing-up or defying it just a little - by not allowing any change at all (over the long years) in his small shop. So, while his shop "Rahim & Sons" remained an unchanging reference point in *Chandni Chowk*[42]; Delhi all around multiplied, grew and metamorphosed at a mind boggling pace. Though un-intended, his adamancy resulted in a kind of reverse publicity for him - as his was now the 'oldest standing' (and visibly so) clock repair shop in Chandni Chowk. And of 'old standing' naturally implied - of high repute as well. Since seeing time never went out of fashion and time pieces never could run without repairs;

---

42 An important market in Old Delhi

he now had customers coming not only from all over Delhi, but from different parts of the country too.

Well into his fifties, his hands were still as sure as a surgeon's. He had from the time he could recollect, spent each day of his life in this shop; surrounded by clocks on each wall. Just as he had grown up helping his grandfather and father in the shop - both his sons now assisted and worked alongside him. Such was his skill, that many a time customers joked - that a clock which hadn't worked for ages; would surprisingly start to tick away the moment placed in Rahim's hands. Anyway, it was a Friday and just after the '*Namaz-e-Jumuah*[43]' as we settled (out of old habit) to share a cup of tea at the Irani Cafe just across the mosque - I lightheartedly asked my friend - If all the clocks in his shop were running on time? Looking up as he sipped from his saucer, he said:

'Clocks you know have a mind of their own and often they make adjustments by themselves; and I have known them long to be able to say that with conviction. I know some lazy folk whose clocks are always running fast; and some hyperactive sorts whose are always running slow - and that no matter how much the timepieces were tinkered with. Some of them are emotional too. Like this watch which once came to me for repairs - where the hour hand, a second before sliding on to four - would jump - and it would be five o' clock; but never four o' clock in that watch. As I got talking to the young lad who had brought it in for repairs - I learnt that it originally belonged to his father - who years before had passed away of a heart attack at four in the evening. Then there was a table clock - which always would run twenty minutes ahead; and if someone tried to

[43] The Friday namaz

set it back, it would simply stop. And believe me nothing was the matter with its springs and coils. And yes, there was a student's alarm clock too - which even if you set the alarm for six in the morning; it would sound up always, without fail, at 4 am. But then I have no complaint. Aren't we humans no different - each with our own whims and idiosyncrasies?

Anyway the ticking of a clock in itself doesn't explain much; just like the sound of a heartbeat - which only goes to prove that one is not yet dead, and nothing more. What is in fact important is not the ticking of time, but – as to what is contained in those moments. Just as the voices of your head are not to be heard in your heartbeat; so is the sound of life not to be found in the ticking of a clock.

Each moment has its own sound - unique and unrepeated; different for different folk. For some it could be a cry, anguish, deep pain or a haunting sorrow while for others the same moment may be one of careless laughter, deep ecstasy, pure happiness or great joy; thus the same wind sounding a different note in each man's flute.

Birth, death, disease and healing - all dancing together in the same moment; each however in its own space. Or say a stone thrown in a pond, creating at the same instant - ripples of a smile, a cry, a promise and a pain. While one laughs the other laments, while one grieves the other celebrates and while one rises the other falls; each man at any moment seeing a different side of the same coin. A garbage bag rides high on the shoulders of a stray wind, a star falls off the night sky, a flower blooms, a tree falls, a cloud sails by and a newly hatched chick falls out of its high nest.

While at close things may appear disjointed, disconnected or strange; but from far it is all as seamless and exact as a perfectly laid mural - with gems of contrasting colours and textures all blending into the one larger picture. A man walking on a street is overtaken by a bicycle, the bicycle by a scooter, the scooter by a car and a plane in the sky above overtakes them all - while an old beggar sitting on the culvert (and going nowhere) quietly watches them pass.

A woman spreads out her laundry on a balcony, a child kicks a stray dog, a couple in the park throw crumbs to the pigeons, a prostitute lures a prospective client, a leper extends his melting hands, an old man pours wheat flour around an ant hill, a mother breast feeds her baby and a butcher prepares to slay his goat. Nothing at all is out of place. This is the final mat being woven - each man like a thread - passing through exactly where he must. All this and more, while the clocks simply tick away in my shop - and their hands keep wiping their tired faces clean'.

"Kya kehte ho, ek ek cup chai aur piyen kya?[44]"

---

[44] What do you say; shall we have another round of tea? (in Hindi)

They Killed It

There was somewhere a very big snake. It was black and no one really knew how long it was. Those who had seen its head could never see its tail; and those who had seen its tail had never seen its head. They were scared and so they decided to kill it. So killing it, they began from one end. They stamped all over it and marched up and down and flattened it out – till it was the level of the ground. They kept it pinned down; lest there is life left and it slips from beneath. Even though their feet grew weary, they continued to tread on it; never leaving it free. Some people, who have seen its head, claim that there's life still left in it and that there's fire in its eyes. If one day it manages to muster its strength, it will shake the men from over its back and slip away into the thick jungle on the other side of the earth. Until then, those who trample upon it are happy to believe that it is dead. And when I asked them the name of this creature; they looked puzzled for a while and then not knowing what to answer, mumbled 'The Road'.

The Gulmohar Tree

It was just across my window and each morning as I sat down with my cup of tea and parted the curtains; the first thing I would see was this Gulmohar tree. While I enjoyed my morning tea – I could see lots of mynahs and other birds hopping around and playing on the branches of the tree and making a volley of chirping sounds. If someday I forgot to part the curtains – this chirping would remind me of the same. Just as one slowly gets used to a friend or a lover, I got used to seeing the Gulmohar and a silent understanding grew between us. It was the season when the Gulmohar had lost the bulk of its canopy and there remained only a few odd green leaves at the branch ends. Despite this, the birds still frequented the tree for the greater part of the day, as if they had entered a lease with the Gulmohar and possessed legal occupancy rights.

The Gulmohar tree was right next to the road within the residential complex where I lived. Over a period of time, I had so structured the route for my morning walks - that I now passed the Gulmohar each morning at a brisk pace. A few of its branches extended a little over the road (as if putting forward a hand of friendship) and there were always a few twigs and petals strewn on this stretch of the walkway. Slowly I got used to the constant presence of the Gulmohar tree in my routine and would like to believe that the Gulmohar too was aware of our growing association.

In a few days heavy rains came down on the city; the initial downpours lasted for about a week and then frequent showers continued over the complete month. During this phase, I missed out quite a bit on my morning walks. And due to the rains, many a mornings I did not part my curtains as well. Some mundane work during this period kept me busy too and as a result I and the Gulmohar didn't see much of each other for some time. You know how life sometimes does not allow any time to idle around with friends?

Then a seminar came along and I had to leave the city for about a fortnight. When I returned, I was astound to note that the Gulmohar was no more the leafless, insipid tree I had seen the last time; this time it was beautiful like a bride, totally loaded with a fiery orange-red blossom and a heavy green canopy of lovely leaves spread out broad like an umbrella.

The Gulmohar tree appeared to be in a different mood altogether and I felt just like one feels to find an old friend altered – happy, but at the same time a little surprised and unsure how the changed friend would behave. But then our association remained unchanged, we communicated with the same ease and understanding as before. I am sure the change was evident to everyone i.e. to the birds, the passersby, and the vehicles driving past.

I once again resumed my morning walks and now could see the Gulmohar's fiery red and orange blossom and its lush canopy every day. Sometimes I picked up a flower and played with it. The birds during this period had a total feast and remained in great celebratory mood which was clearly visible. I think they found the young leaves and the tender buds of the Gulmohar an exotic delicacy. They seemed to have more energy than before and the pitch of their chirping was definitely several notches higher.

At night while everything was dark outside and as I worked silently in the light of my table lamp, I had a kind of reassuring feeling that even though I couldn't see it in the dark, the Gulmohar tree was always there across my window. The Gulmohar over the next few months was a constant presence in my life; just like a pet that is always there even if you are busy and don't have much time for it.

Time passed and life went on without much ado. One day, dark clouds started building up right from the morning; slowly by afternoon the sky became all packed and ominous. There was no wind, everything lay still and there was a strange silence. It quite seemed like a lull before the storm. By evening it was certain that a heavy rain would break out soon. However the weather held still, its foreboding mood continuing well into the night. Finally around midnight, the weather let loose. It seemed like a hurricane with lashing winds. I heard glass window panes shatter, tin roofs being blown off and doors banging. It was a fury I had never witnessed before. I think this violent storm with howling winds lasted almost about two hours and then gave way to a heavy rain. The kind of rain that is violent too; which doesn't fall but hits hard at everything. So it was this kind of stuff that carried on well into the night that day. Towards the early hours of the morning, the storm waned and that is when I guess, I fell asleep.

At about seven in the morning I woke up to the sound of a heavy truck revving its engine on the road below and heard several loud voices. Slowly I got up, groggy with sleep and walked to the balcony to check what this commotion was all about. There were stray leaves littered on the balcony and glass lay shattered from the windows above. An electric pole had crashed over a parked car and its steel wires lay snapped like thread. And flower pots from my balcony - with beautiful yellow and white chrysanthemums lay smashed in the parking lot below.

It was then that I noticed another activity, this time a little further away; ahead of my compound and across the road. There I noticed a yellow truck of the town municipality and eight to ten men trying to haul up a heavy load onto the truck. Some heavy object on the ground appeared to have been tied with thick ropes. While few men inside the body of the truck were trying to pull up this load with the ropes, a few below were trying to lift it up into the truck. Since I was not wearing my glasses I could not clearly make out the object, but it was evident that the load was pretty heavy. They shouted across to each other to coordinate their efforts.

And then with a thud inside my chest, it came to me that this exactly was the place where the Gulmohar tree had always stood. With a sinking feeling and tightness in my throat I noticed that the Gulmohar tree was no longer to be seen, where it once stood majestically. And then I could see that it was the Gulmohar tree which this group of men was trying to haul up into their truck. My mouth all of a sudden went dry and I sensed a strange nausea. In the next few minutes the men pulled and pushed, and lifted the Gulmohar tree into the truck and drove away; unceremoniously without a care (perhaps to lift more of such trees which had fallen elsewhere in the town).

Something had changed. There was now just a vacant space where till the previous evening the Gulmohar had elegantly stood. As I drove for work that day (a little late than other days); and as I drove past the spot where the Gulmohar once used to be - I noticed some red upturned soil and a few of its leaves and flowers still scattered around. The traffic was plying as usual on the road; everyone was in the same hurry to get to nowhere. But for me, something had changed forever. A portion of my life was irreparably severed. Something vital had gone out of my veins. The days that followed were never the same. I gave up parting my curtains in the morning. The birds also never made as much a noise as before. And though I have seen many Gulmohar trees in other places since then; but they were not the same. They were not like the one that perished and went away.

Welcome...

(What it could come to one day)

Welcome! to the world of reading. For reading in Hindi, go to the index on page number 2. For reading in English, go to the index on page number 3. For Spanish, Latin, German, French or other foreign languages, please refer to the indices from page numbers 4 to 11. For reading in any of the regional Indian languages - turn to page numbers 12 to 22. If you would like to read on financial issues or subjects pertaining to investment in equity, mutual funds or government bonds - please scan and mail your *PAN*[45] number and *Aadhar Card*[46] to the email as mentioned on page number 23. For reading on crime and murder mysteries - please forward your mental health certificate and copy of your police verification (or history sheet) a

---

45 Permanent Account Number (PAN) is a code that acts as identification of Indians who pay Income Tax

46 Is a proof of identity and address anywhere in India

week in advance to the distributor's office - the address is as printed on the left hand corner of the back cover.

For reading on erotica or on subjects related to sex, sexual health, sexual practices or erogenous obsessions - please indicate whether you are lesbian, gay, bisexual or transgender; and also authenticate your adulthood by mailing a copy of your birth certificate or high school passing certificate to the address as mentioned at page number 24.

To read on issues related to automobiles i.e. that is cars, scooters, motorbikes etc. or on Formula 1 Racing - prior receipt of your valid driving license and vehicle registration number is obligatory.

To read in font sizes 48 to 65, please refer page numbers 25 to 225. For reading in font sizes greater than 65 - please ensure that your vision is intact; or else refer to the braille section from page numbers 226 to 448. For people who are blind as well as have lost their hands in accidents - you may tune in your head phones (with help from your neighbors or nurse) to the audio books at page numbers 449 to 522. For people who are squint - we have special stories at page numbers 523 to 868; where the left page text is printed on the right and the right page text is printed on the left.

If you want to read the selected book today, tomorrow, day after or the day day after – please subscribe and order the book accordingly. Do not read yesterday's book today or tomorrow's chapters yesterday. Confusion, ill health, physical injury or mental disorders so caused, by such confusion, shall be the sole liability of the reader. Any representation on such account if referred would be entirely ignored by the publishers.

For those in the habit of reading fast or pressed for time; but still wanting to savour the joy of having read it all - please refer to the special quick reading editions at page numbers 869 to 1261. Volume I of the edition has only the odd words printed in the novel; that is from the original unabridged version - words placed at chronological sequences 1,3,5,7,9,11,13 and so on. While Volume II is the even version; that is where only the words 2,4,8,10,12,14 and so on are printed. These editions naturally are half in volume to the original version. In large offices and corporate houses such reading has been found to be most cost effective and organization friendly. Here the readers of Volumes I and II have been observed filling-in the blanks and covering each other's gaps during the coffee and lunch breaks. Besides minimizing the man hours spent reading, this also minimizes idle gossip and bickering over management high-handedness.

If you are more of a do-it-yourself kind of person, or say wanting to read along with writing, you may go to pages 1262 and onwards. Here you will find short stories and novellas where only the alternate paragraphs have been printed; with adequate blank spaces left in-between for writing of the missing story. This will allow you to add your very own twists and idiosyncrasies as you go along. You however would need to adhere to the word limit for each paragraph. And introduce only up to a maximum of three new characters into the story, if found inescapable. The characters so inserted (if at all) must maintain the sanctity of the main plot and be prevented (at all costs) from murdering, marrying, kidnapping or sodomizing any of the original characters. And of course the final readability (or otherwise) of the finished story - shall rest half with you.

To go back to the main menu or index - go to page number 1. For talking to any of our literary agents, dial the toll free numbers given at the bottom of the back cover. And thanks for choosing this book. We appreciate your interest. A record of what you read or browse may be maintained for future reference.

However, since you have taken more than the stipulated time for making your choice - your right to read this book is hereby forfeited. This book will self-destruct in the next ten seconds. Ten, nine, eight, seven.........

Printed in the United States
By Bookmasters